SCI-FI JUNIOR HIGH

JOHN MARTIN   SCOTT SEEGERT

SCHOLASTIC

Scholastic Children's Books
An imprint of Scholastic Ltd
Euston House, 24 Eversholt Street, London, NW1 1DB, UK
Registered office: Westfield Road, Southam, Warwickshire, CV47 0RA
SCHOLASTIC and associated logos are trademarks and/or
registered trademarks of Scholastic Inc.

First published in the US by Jimmy Patterson Books/Little, Brown and
Company, 2017
First published in the UK by Scholastic Ltd, 2017

ISBN 978 1407 17993 3

A CIP catalogue record for this book
is available from the British Library.

Printed by CPI Group (UK) Ltd, Croydon, CR0 4YY
Papers used by Scholastic Children's Books are made
from wood grown in sustainable forests.

1 3 5 7 9 10 8 6 4 2

www.scholastic.co.uk

To the true Mighty Mega
Supergeniuses of our youth:

Stan Lee, Jack Kirby, the Incredible Hulk,
Spider-man, Batman, Dr. Doom, Godzilla,
Mothra, Ghidorah, Frankenstein, the Wolf Man,
Moe, Larry, Curly, Shemp, Daffy Duck, Yosemite
Sam, Mel Blanc, Chuck Jones, Scooby-Doo,
Shaggy, Herman, Lily, Grandpa, Don Martin,
Sergio Aragonés, Vincent Price, Christopher
Lee, the Ghoul, Space Ghost, Zorak, Raquel
Welch, Chewbacca, Frank Frazetta, Big Daddy
Roth, Jonny Quest, Mr. Spock, Captain Kirk,
Will Robinson, the Robot, Dr. Smith, the
Herculoids, Adam West, Burt Ward, and all the
rest we don't have space to mention. You helped
make us what we are today. And our wives
would like to have a word with you.

FOREWORD

Sci-Fi Junior High is about a new kid named Kelvin, whose school happens to be in space. Weird, right? But that's what makes reading so great— you get to explore weird and wonderful ideas like crime-fighting turtles, secret schools for wizards, and a flying boy who never wants to grow up.

And just like Kelvin, you might find something fantastically "weird" in these pages: a book that's *fun* to read. *Sci-Fi Junior High* has spaceships, robots, mad scientists, aliens, bullies, new friends, and hilarious comic art. You'll laugh so loud they'll hear you on the moon. And at the end, just like with all our JIMMY books, you'll want to say, "Please, give me another book!"

Wouldn't that be weird?

—James Patterson

Prologue

WHAT'S THIS?! A YOUNG HUMAN? AT THE FAR END OF THE GALAXY? IN SOME DEEP-SPACE DOO-DOO?!

WOAAHHHHHHHH!!!
WHAT HAVE I GOTTEN MYSELF INTO?
GOOD QUESTION! LET'S FIND OUT.

A few days earlier . . .

DAY 1

Seriously? Mom and Dad expect me to get up and go to school the morning after a 329,000,000,000,000,000-mile road trip across the galaxy? And I'm not even a morning person to begin with. I can't fake being sick, either. Not with the sterile environment of the space station. No germs = no sickness. Ever. Not even the sniffles. At least I got a good night's sleep. The zero-gravity pods in our LIV spaces are waaaay more comfortable than regular beds. And you can sleep standing up, so they take up less space.

Oh, hold on a second. I guess I should explain. My name is Kelvin, and I'm about to start my first day at a new school, which is nothing new to me. Our family moves around a lot, and this is my fourth new school in the past five years. It's just that this one is 56,000 light-years from the last one.

And this is my family. My mom and dad are scientists, really smart ones, which is why we're moving around all the time. They keep getting new projects to work on, and we have to go where the projects are. In this case, that's the other end of the galaxy. Oh, and down on the end there is my little sister, Bula. Unfortunately, she had to come along with us. So I guess there really is one germ on this space station.

Robotics is Dad's specialty. You may already be familiar with some of his work. Like the X9000 PulverBot he designed for Global Mining, Inc.

Then there's the PL370 Rootin' Tootin' Asteroid-Shootin' Bot he created to keep foreign objects from colliding with the earth.

And, of course, the NIVEN6000 All-Terrain Fully Armoured Nuclear-Powered Rescue/Bake Bot . . .

Dad feels that anyone in dire need of rescue must also be in dire need of a warm, freshly baked chocolate chip cookie.

Then there's my mom. She's a neuroscientist, which means she plays around with brains.

No, not like that. She works with the brains while they're still inside the heads. At least, that's what she tells me. Although it would be pretty cool to have an evil scientist for a mom!

Since my mom and dad are both super-geniuses, that obviously makes me a supergenius, too, right? Nope. It makes me a double super-genius! Or what I like to call a Mighty Mega Supergenius! It also makes me the smartest human being in the world. There's really no arguing the fact. It's simple maths.

And this is our new "home". . .

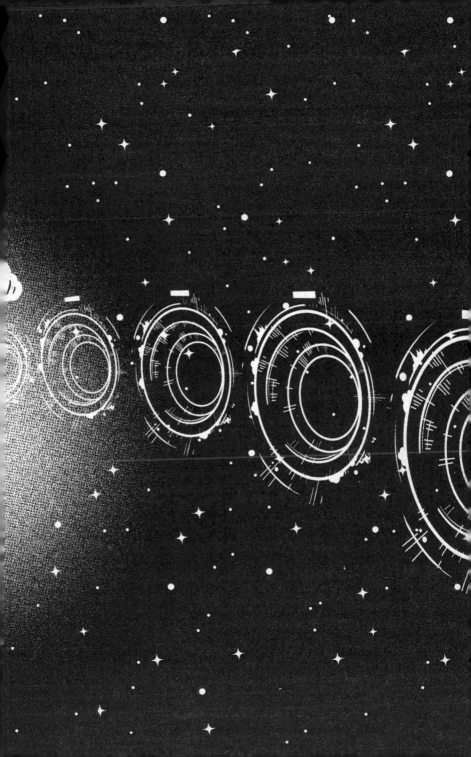

It's called the Galactic Science Hub. The top two scientists from more than two hundred different planets live aboard it with their families. So do all the other workers and their families. It's huge, it's in the middle of space, and it's the first place I've ever lived *aboard* instead of in.

We haven't even been here a day yet, but like I said, the zero-gravity pods are awesome. The "showers," though—not so much. We have to be careful how much water we use on the space station, so we clean up using this thing called a Vacuu-Suk 3000.

Sure, it sucks all the dirt off your body. It even sucks all the dirt off your clothes. But no way is it as relaxing as a hot shower. Plus, you have to hold your breath for fifteen seconds. Plus, you really have to work the hair gel when you're done.

But so far so good, I guess.

Most days I'll take the shuttle bus over to the school they set up for all the kids on the Science Hub. It's sort of its own separate mini space station. Fortunately, the older kids have their own school, so we don't have to deal with them very often. Even better, the little kids, like Bula, stay aboard the Science Hub and out of our hair.

Since it's my first day, though, Mom is taking me in. Normally, this would be a major bag-over-the-head situation, but I get to go in a little late so we can meet with Principal Ort before I go to class. I figure the hallways should be mostly empty if we get there before class lets out, so as long as I keep my head down and slink along the walls, no one should see us together.

"C'mon, Mom!" I yell. "I don't want to be late for my meeting!"

"I'll just be a minute," she yells back from the bathroom. "I think it's great that you're so excited to get started at your new school, Kelvin!"

"Actually, not so much excited as worried that hundreds of kids' first impressions of me will be the dweeb who has to have his mommy bring him to school," I say. Very quietly. To myself. Nothing could be worse.

"Okay, Kelvin. I'm ready to go."

Okay . . . this is worse.

"Uh . . . Mom?" I say. "Your . . . umm . . . hair is . . ."

"I know! Isn't it wonderful? And I didn't even have to do anything to get it this way! I just love that Vacuu-Suk 3000!"

Please, please, please can we get to school before class lets out?

So this is it. Sciriustrati Fibronoculareus Junior High School.

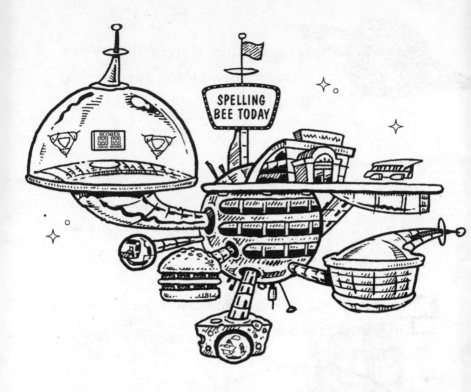

I'm not really sure how to pronounce it, but Dad said everybody just calls it Sci-Fi Junior High. The whole way over here I've been trying to come up with a plan to keep Mom from coming in to school with me. And I think I've got it! All I need is a flashlight, a jet pack, three gallons of blueberry yoghurt, forty feet of high-strength fishing line, and a bucket of . . .

 "You know what, Kelvin? Why don't you just go ahead into your meeting without me?"

. . . golf balls.

 "I'm sure the last thing you need is to be seen with your mom on your first day, right?"

KLOMP!

SPLink

"I'll just stop in and talk to the principal later this afternoon. Have a great day. Oh, and don't forget your helmet."

I can't believe it! It worked! My plan actually worked! And I didn't even have to . . . you know . . . use it! Now to play it cool. I don't want to seem too happy she's not coming in and hurt her feelings.

"You sure, Mom? It's really not a big deal."

"Really? Well, in that case I suppose I could stop in for a minute or two and—"

"NO! I mean . . . you don't have to do that. I . . . I'm sure you're real busy with . . . whatever it is you're working on. I'll be fine."

Yikes. Now I kinda wish she *was* here. Starting at a new school . . . with a weird name . . . in the middle of outer space? What was I thinking wanting to do this by myself? What if the articificial gravity on this platform stops working? What if I accidentally open the wrong door and get sucked out an air lock? What if my helmet cracks and my head implodes while I'm standing out here thinking about all the horrible things that could happen?

I'd better get inside.

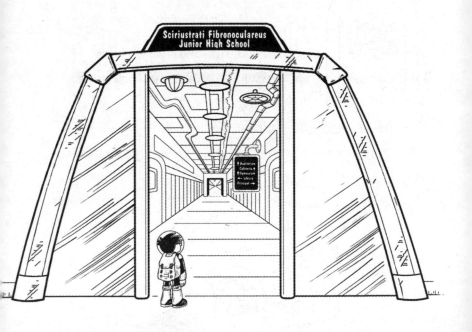

I sure hope Principal Ort is in his office. Or is it her office? Guess I'll find out soon enough.

This looks like it. I press the button on the door.

· PRINCIPAL ORT ·

"It's Kelvin Klosmo," I say. "I'm a new student and—"

"Ah, yes!" the eyeball interrupts. "Mr. Klosmo! Come right in and have a seat. We've been expecting you."

The door slides open and I step inside.

Hmm. Still no idea whether he is a she . . . or she is a he. Or both. Or neither.

 "Hello, Kelvin. My name is Principal Ort, and I must say that we are very pleased to have you here at Sciriustrati Fibronoculareus Junior High School. VERY pleased! TREMENDOUSLY pleased! EXTRAORDINARILY pleased!"

 "Wow. Thanks, I guess. But how do you even know who I am?"

 "Who you are? Why, you're Kelvin Klosmo—the only student in the entire school who has both parents serving as scientists on the space station. Which means, of course, that your parents are the two most brilliant scientific minds on your entire planet. I can't even imagine

what a genius you must be! We're expecting incredible things from you, young man. INCREDIBLE things! MAGNIFICENT things! SPLENDIFEROUS things!"

Uh-oh. Splendiferous? I don't even know what that means. You know that Mighty Mega Supergeniusness I told you about before? Well, I wasn't being totally honest. I sort of forgot to mention that it hasn't actually, you know, kicked in yet. It's still stuck somewhere in the back of my brain, waiting for the right time to show itself. But I'm positive it's only a matter of time. And I'm guessing it should happen pretty soon. Probably at the same time my voice changes. Only it's going to hit me all at once, like some massive bolt of lightning. Or a nuclear explosion. I just hope I'm not going to the bathroom when it happens! Until then I've got to keep faking it. Sometimes it feels like my being a genius is the only reason anyone even notices me at school.

"Uh . . . well . . . I'm expecting big things from me, too. I guess."

 "Excellent! Now, where did I put your class schedule? Ah. Here it is. Let me just put on my reading glasses and take a look at which classroom you should be in at the moment."

"Ah. There we go. Now let's see . . . yes, here we are. Eleven twenty a.m. You should be having lunch in the cafeteria. And what an excellent way to begin your first day. Lunch Lady LL7000 always serves up delicious meals. DELICIOUS meals! DE-

LECTIBLE meals! MELT-IN-YOUR-
MOUTH meals! Let's go. I'll show you
the way."

As we get up to leave, I notice a picture frame
on the desk. Maybe this will help me figure out if
Principal Ort is a Mr. or a Mrs. Or a Miss. Or a Mx.

"Is that your family, Principal Ort?"

 "Why, yes it is, Kelvin. How nice
of you to ask. We've been happily
married for one hundred thirty-six
years. And we have a wonderful son
and daughter. We're both so proud."

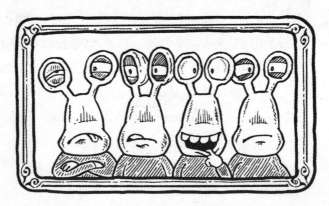

Nope. No help there. Principal Ort leads me down the deserted hallway to the cafeteria. "Well, here's where I leave you for now," he or she says. "Have a wonderful first day, Kelvin. A WONDERFUL day! A SPECTACULAR day! A SENSATIONAL day! I'm extremely excited to see what great things you accomplish here."

And then it's just me—and the cafeteria door.

Well, here goes nothing. What do I have to be afraid of, anyway? I've been to plenty of new schools. I mean, how different could this one really be?

4

"Hmmm. I don't remember seeing you before."

"It's my first day."

'Really? What planet are you from?"

"Earth."

 "Do they teach you how to duck on Earth?"

"What? Why?"

INCOMING!

FLOOSH!

 "C'mon, let's get out of the line of fire."

"So, what's going on? Does this happen a lot around here?"

 "Every once in a while. It usually starts with some misunderstanding. Like today—somebody mistook another student for a dessert and covered him with whipped gream. That's when all shnort broke loose.

In his defence, though, the kid does look an awful lot like Jell-O."

Oh man. My Mighty Mega Supergeniusness better kick in soon, or I'm in for a loooong year.

"I guess my, uh, reputation precedes me."

"It sure did. But now that you're here, it can just show up the same time you do from now on. Hey, say something brilliant!"

"Brilliant? Like what?"

"How would I know? You're the genius."

Yikes! Being put on the spot already. Think, Kelvin. There must be some smart, interesting factoid you can drum up. Something? Anything? Just as I'm about to tell Spotch that the capital of Vermont is Montpelier, Principal Ort comes through the cafeteria door.

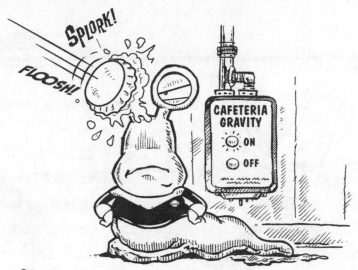

 "Uh-oh. Better grab hold of something quick!"

"What? Why?"

45

Okay, no more questioning Spotch. I'm just going to do whatever he tells me to from now on. On the bright side, Principal Ort just saved me from completely embarrassing myself. "Well," he (or she) says, "this is certainly an awful mess. An AWFUL mess! A TERRIBLE mess! An INEXCUSABLE mess! You will all report to your next class immediately. No gymnasium time for any of you after this little stunt. Now off you go!"

"Better brace yourself."

"What? Why?"

47

For the smartest kid in the galaxy, I sure am a slow learner.

Well, that was quite a start to my new school career. In the first twenty minutes alone I learned to:

1. Take Spotch's advice.
2. Never count on there being gravity.
3. Be careful not to accidentally eat a classmate for dessert.

I guess I could also add "never hit your principal in the eyestalk with a pie." Not that I was the one who did it, but still something to remember. It's all good, though, because I also met my first new friend. Even better, it turns out that Spotch and I have the same schedule after lunch. So after picking the pieces of fried glorp cheese out of my hair, I walk with him to Mr. Jeddee's science class.

Mr. Jeddee introduces me to the class. I hear some murmuring from the students.

"That's him!"

"Wow! THE Kelvin Klosmo!"

"He doesn't look that smart."

He assigns me to Spotch's table, where six kids are already sitting.

I grab Spotch before he can sit down.

"Hey—could you fill me in on my tablemates?"

I ask him. "I think it might be a good idea if I knew a little about them before we meet. You know, so I'm not accidentally rude or something."

"Sure thing," Spotch says. "Seems logical."

RAND-EL IS SORT OF OUR GROUP PESSIMIST. I GUESS I MIGHT BE, TOO, IF I WAS THE ONLY ONE ON MY ENTIRE PLANET WHO HAD TO WEAR GLASSES. IF YOU REALLY WANT TO GET UNDER HIS SKIN, CALL HIM "TWELVE EYES." HE HATES THAT.

GIL LAGOONIE COMES FROM AN OCEAN PLANET WHERE EVERYBODY LIVES UNDERWATER. WHILE HE'S HERE, HE HAS TO STAY IN A PORTABLE FISH BOWL ALL THE TIME. HE SEEMS TO DO OKAY WITH IT, BUT I DON'T EVEN WANT TO KNOW WHERE HE GOES TO THE BATHROOM.

ZOT TOTZIE IS VERY...PEPPY. AND ENERGETIC. SHE COULD HAVE STOPPED WEARING BRACES FOUR YEARS AGO, BUT SHE SAYS SHE LIKES HOW THEY MAKE HER SMILE "SPARKLE." I DON'T EVEN KNOW IF HER LIPS CAN CLOSE. AND I COULD BE WRONG, BUT IT LOOKS LIKE SHE HAS A CRUSH ON YOU.

GRIMNEE AND ZOT ARE BFFS. GRIMNEE'S PRETTY QUIET. HER HOME PLANET IS ENORMOUS, WITH MANY TIMES THE GRAVITY OF A TYPICAL PLANET, SO SHE'S REALLY STRONG COMPARED TO EVERYBODY ELSE ON THE SPACE STATION. TRUST ME— YOU DO NOT WANT TO GET ON HER BAD SIDE.

BRIAN STEM IS THE MOST INTELLIGENT KID IN THE ENTIRE SCHOOL. AT LEAST HE WAS BEFORE YOU SHOWED UP. HE'S ALSO THE LEAST INTELLIGENT. AND EVERYTHING IN BETWEEN. HIS BRAIN CHANGES SIZES DEPENDING ON HOW NERVOUS HE IS—THE MORE STRESSED OUT HE GETS, THE SMALLER HIS BRAIN BECOMES. AND HE GETS STRESSED OUT PRETTY EASILY. OH, AND HE REALLY LIKES PUDDING.

MIPPITT IS ANOTHER NEW KID, LIKE YOU. HE'S ONLY BEEN IN OUR GROUP SINCE YESTERDAY. WE DON'T KNOW MUCH ABOUT HIM YET BECAUSE HE'S NOT REAL TALKATIVE. ACTUALLY, I'VE NEVER HEARD HIM SAY A WORD. HE DOES MAKE A HIGH-PITCHED HUM EVERY NOW AND THEN, THOUGH.

Yikes! Back on Earth, I thought Teddy Krumlets was strange because he used to eat the shavings out of the pencil sharpener. But this is a whole other thing altogether.

Wow. What a first day. And to think—yesterday morning I woke up in my own bed, in my own house, in my own solar system. You're probably wondering how I actually got here, to this hunk of metal floating around in deep space. And I should probably tell you about it while it's all still fresh in my mind. Who knows what'll happen when my Mighty Mega Supergeniusness kicks in. It might even scramble my memories a bit, and I want to make sure you get the whole, true story.

So, there we were, hurtling through space in our transport shuttle.

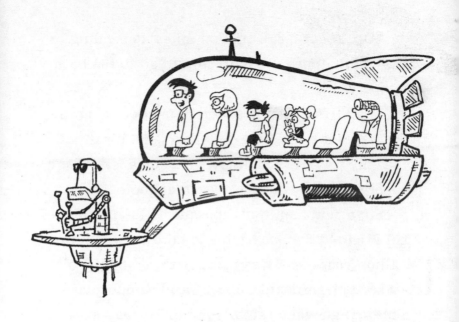

We had another passenger in the back, sort of a frail old guy. I had no idea who he was.

But I did have an idea of just how far we had to travel to get to the space station—56,000 light-years! Do you have any idea how far that is? Me either. At least, I didn't before I asked my dad.

"Well, son, a light-year is the distance that light can travel in one year."

"And how far is that, Dad?"

"Oh, about 5.878 trillion miles, depending on how many times it has to stop to go to the bathroom. HAR!"

That "HAR" is the sound of my dad laughing. He makes it every time he tells a joke. It's usually the only way we even know he made a joke. For a supergenius, my dad can be a real goofball.

So, a few hundred thousand trillion miles to go? I figured that was going to take a few hundred trillion years, so I was pretty sure I'd be the oldest seventh grader at Sciriustrati Fibronoculareus Junior High when I finally got there. Maybe there was a shortcut?

"Uh, Dad?" I asked. "How much longer till we get there?"

"Well, we still have about forty-five minutes before we reach the wormhole on the back side of the moon. After that I'd say twenty-seven seconds and we'll be at the far side of the galaxy. Twenty-nine if we run into traffic. HAR!"

Another joke. But a shortcut, too!

"Wormhole?" I asked.

"That's right. You do know what a wormhole is, don't you, Kelvin?"

"Uhh . . . oh, a wormhole. Of course I know what that is."

I had no idea what that was. Wormhole? Seriously? Never heard of it. But I couldn't let my parents know that. I'd done a pretty good job of hiding the fact that my superbrilliance hadn't risen to the surface yet. I'd hate to blow it now and disappoint them.

Besides, there were really only three things it could possibly be, right?

WORMHOLE POSSIBILITY 1— A hole that a worm made. Like in an apple. Not sure how that would help get us across the galaxy in twenty-seven seconds, though. Maybe it was a magic apple, and when you ate the part with the hole in it, you were instantly transported bazillions of miles across the galaxy. Hmm. Seemed reasonable.

 **WORMHOLE POSSIBILITY 2**— A hole in the ground filled with worms. You held your breath, jumped in the hole, and . . . ZWAP! You were on the other side of the galaxy. Definitely a possibility.

 **WORMHOLE POSSIBILITY 3**— A hole in a worm. Hey— now we were getting somewhere! It would have to be a giant worm, so the hole would be big enough to climb into. Then the worm would do a wicked-fast space crawl to the far side of the galaxy. Kind of gross, but yeah, that must be what it was. Come to think of it, my first two ideas seemed sort of ridiculous now.

"Hey, everyone," Dad said. "We're at the wormhole!"

"Wait a minute," I said. "Where's the ginormous worm? Did it already go through the hole?"

"HAR! Did you hear that, hon?" said Dad. " Pretending to confuse a bridge across space-time with a gigantic limbless invertebrate!"

"He's always had a wonderful sense of humour, that one!" Mom added.

A bridge across space-time? So, no actual worm? Man, it was getting harder and harder to fake being a Mighty Mega Supergenius.

What the . . . ?

Okay. Either I was having space-travel-induced butt spasms or somebody was kicking the back of my seat. I turned around to see what was what.

Ugh. It was that annoying, goofy-looking little creature.

And she was holding her stuffed animal.

Me hogging all the brains passed down from our parents meant there wasn't much left over for my little sister, Bula.

At least, that's what I imagine it must look like in there. Here, I'll give you an example of what I'm talking about.

 "Hey, Bula. What's eighteen divided by three?"

"Ummmmm . . . I dunno."

See? Nothing going on inside that pigtailed

little skull of hers. I think the hamster might even have died.

 "It's six, Bula. How do you not know that?"

"Umm, because I'm only four? And at least I know a wormhole isn't in a real worm."

 "THAT WAS A JOKE! I obviously knew what a wormhole was."

"No, you didn't."

 "Yes, I did!"

"Nope."

 "Yes, I . . . why am I even arguing with you about this?"

"Because you didn't know what a wormhole was."

 "Yes, I did! And that's it! I'm done arguing!"

 "You didn't know what a wormhole was. You didn't know what a wormhole was."

 "Yes, I did!"

"Nope."

 "Yup!"

Zarfloots! Why didn't they give me my own private shuttle? This is going to be the longest 329-quadrillion-mile trip ever—even if it does last only twenty-seven seconds. It's enough to make my stomach churn! Which reminds me . . . I'm hungry.

Double zarfloots! Children and space travel make a horrible combination. Come to think of it, children and anything make a horrible combination. Because of the children part. They're just so . . . yuck.

Especially these children, since they belong to those infernal Klosmos. Those two have been robbing me, Erik Failenheimer, of my glory for longer than I can remember. So Klyde Klosmo designed a robot to destroy asteroids headed toward Earth. Big whoop. So did I.

Okay, so mine had a few glitches, but nothing a few thousand minor adjustments couldn't have taken care of. But did they give me a chance? Nooooooooooo! They just used Klosmo's bot instead. They always choose the Klosmos. For everything!

But now, at last, things will be different! The top scientists from all over the galaxy are being brought together at the Galactic Science Hub to work on a top secret project. This is my chance to show what brilliance I am capable of! This is my chance to finally gain the respect that Erik Failenheimer so richly deserves!

"So, where are you folks headed?"

"To the Galactic Science Hub."

 "Oh, I doubt that."

"What do you mean? Won't this wormhole take us there?"

 "Darn right it'll take you there. It's the only place it'll take you. One entrance, one exit. That's how a wormhole works, you know."

"Of course I know. Everyone knows how a wormhole works."

"So, what's the problem, exactly?"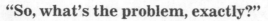

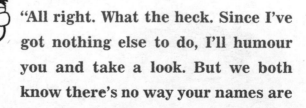

"The problem, exactly, is that for you to go through this here wormhole, I'd have to let you through this here gate. And for me to let you through this here gate, your names would have to be on THE LIST. And THE LIST is very short. So short, in fact, that I've been sitting here for three and a half years and nobody's gone through yet."

"Well, I'm Professor Klyde Klosmo and this is my wife, Professor Klara Klosmo. And these are our children, Kelvin and Bula."

"All right. What the heck. Since I've got nothing else to do, I'll humour you and take a look. But we both know there's no way your names are on the . . . well, I'll be a wallaby's earlobe! You folks really are on THE LIST."

"Great. Now let's get going. You've wasted enough of my precious time."

"And just who might you be?"

"Who might I be?! I might be Harry Potter! I might be Peter Pan!"

"Sorry, pal. Neither of those names is on THE LIST."

"Of course they're not on the list! They aren't even real peop—never mind! Do you really not recognize the world-renowned Professor Erik M. Failenheimer when you see him?!"

"Nope. And I don't see that name on THE LIST, either."

"Well, look again! I was specifi-cally invited!"

 "All right, but I don't see how I could have missed . . . well, what do you know. Here you are . . . at the very bottom. After Mr. Fluffles."

"Mr. Fluffles? Who's Mr. Fluffles?"

"A plushy?! I'm listed after a plushy?!"

"Look, mister. I didn't make THE LIST. I just make sure you're on it. And you are. Which means you folks are cleared to go. Have a nice trip."

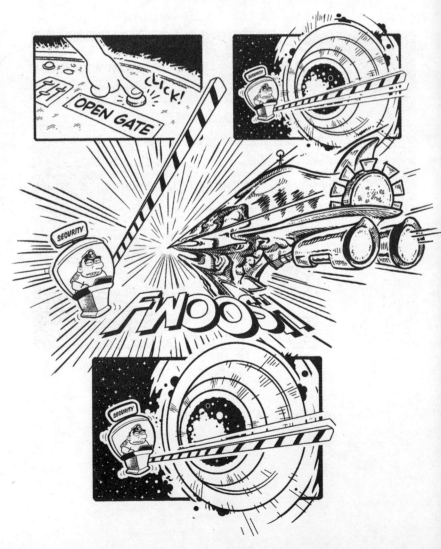

hoa! Now I knew what a wormhole was—
AWESOME! Crazy lights flashing all over
the place. Everybody looking all weirded out and
goofy. Of course, that was nothing new for Bula.

I felt like Silly Putty in a juice blender!

Yikes! I guess old skin takes a little longer to snap back into shape.

"All right, everyone," Dad said, "we're here! Halfway across the galaxy in less time than it takes Dr. Hackersham to comb his hair in the morning. HAR!"

Dr. Hackersham is our dentist. He's also bald. Get it? It looked like 56,000 light-years hadn't improved Dad's sense of humour any.

"And there it is," Dad said, beaming. "Right in front of us—the Galactic Science Hub! Isn't she a beaut?"

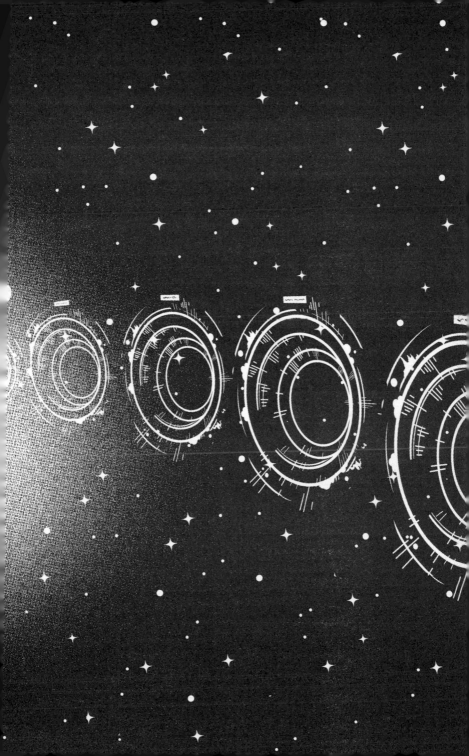

Mom's eyes were wide open. "My goodness," she said. "It's even more impressive than I thought it would be! Simply marvellous! I can't wait to settle in and get to work."

"By the way, just what exactly is your work, anyway?" I asked. "What's so important that someone who builds robots and someone who studies brains have to drag their whole family all the way out here?"

"Well, son," Dad started to explain, "your mother and I will be working on an extremely important project to retrieve a—OUCH!"

I noticed Mom's fingernails digging into Dad's forearm. She didn't look happy.

"That is," Dad continued, his eyes watering slightly, "an extremely important project to make . . . uh . . . smarter robots!"

He looked over at Mom, eyebrows raised.

"You know, so they can be more useful to us around the house and run errands and such."

Mom let go of Dad's arm. He rubbed the welts and let out a sigh of relief. That was . . . weird.

"That's all we can say for now," Mom said. "Let's give you a few days to settle in at your new school, and then your dad and I can tell you all about it. How does that sound?"

The part about robots doing my chores sounded ... strange ... but also awesome! The part about starting all over at a new school in deep space—not so much. The smartest kid in the world would be up for the challenge, though, so I put on my bravest face.

"Sounds awesome! Can't wait to get started!"

"Great!" Dad replied. "I just know you're going to love it here, Kelvin. Well, what are we waiting for, driver? Let's go!"

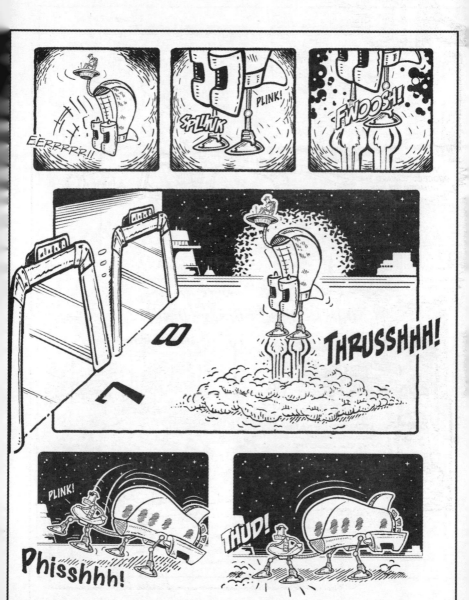

ow. The landing bay of the space station was
the biggest thing I'd ever been in in my life! I
couldn't even see all the way to the far end. And it
was loaded with shuttles just like ours. There must
have been hundreds of them. And lots of other
ships, too. Some looked barely big enough to hold

one person, but most of them seemed large enough to carry a whole bunch of passengers. And equipment, too. Weird things. Like the kind of stuff my dad would come up with.

 "If you'll follow me, folks, I'll take you to your living quarters. But first you'll need to remove your clothing."

"Please, sir. Not out here. I'll show you to the changing area, where you'll find a new uniform with your name on it. You can toss your old clothes in the marked disposal bin."

Uniform? Wait a minute—nobody ever mentioned anything about a uniform! I really liked the clothes I already had. It took a lot of effort to look that good. And I really didn't want to start out at a new school wearing some dorky uniform. I asked Dad what the deal was.

"Contamination, son. Contamination. There are many different species from many different planets aboard the Science Hub, and germs that might be harmless to you and me could prove disastrous to someone else. And vice versa. There's no telling what the effects could be. You wouldn't want to be brushing your teeth and have your head fall off into the sink, now would you?"

"No. I guess not." Head fall off? Into the sink? And no "HAR!" at the end? Holy cow, he might actually have been serious! I quickly changed into my new outfit, sadly tossed my ultracool stud duds into the bin, and met everyone back outside the changing rooms.

Hey, you know what? The uniforms weren't half bad! In fact, they were so sweet they could probably make anybody look good.

Well . . .

All right! Enough is enough! First the shuttle and now . . . this?! Where's the respect?

 "Look here! Somebody's made a mistake! My uniform doesn't look anything like the Klosmos'."

"A mistake? And your name is . . . ?"

 "Failenheimer! Professor Erik M. Failenheimer!"

"Well, then, this is your uniform, all right. Says so right on the name tag."

 "Well, why does his say 'Professor Klyde Klosmo'?"

"Because that's his name, I would assume."

"Has been since I was born! HAR!"

 "I mean, why does mine just say 'Erik'? Something is obviously miss-ing."

"Well, let's take a look-see at the assignment sheet. Failen-heimer . . . ah, here you are. And you're right. There does appear to be something missing."

 "Well . . . that's better!"

 "A mop?!"

 "It says right here: 'All custodians will be assigned sterilized, germ-free cleaning equipment immediately upon changing into their new uniform.' I'm sorry. I missed that the first time around."

 "Custodian?! I'll have you know I came in third place in the most recent Scientist of the Year competition for the entire planet Earth!"

 "Well, good for you. Unfortunately, only the top two scientists from each planet are invited to continue their research here on the Galactic Science Hub. You shouldn't feel bad, though. All of our custodians have been selected based upon their scientific knowledge as well. After all, you never know what type of hazardous messes you may have to clean up."

Hazardous shmazardous! This is the last straw. The world won't have Erik Failenheimer to kick around anymore. If they won't respect me as a brilliant scientist, maybe they will respect me as a brilliantly EVIL scientist! Yes, that's it! I'll be patient until I figure out what's so important about this space station, and then I'll take it for myself! Take it and use it to become the MOST POWERFUL BEING ON EARTH! IN THE GALAXY! IN THE UNIVERSE!

DAY 2

Okay. So that was my trip across the galaxy. I tried my best to describe it, but trust me, it was waaaayyyy cooler than I could even make it sound! At least it's down on paper, though, in case my memory gets fuzzy later on. Come to think of it, I probably should have left the parts about Bula out. The less of her in my memory, the better.

But back to what's going on now—my science class just took a shuttle bus back to the space station for a field trip. I say "back" since that's where our LIV spaces are and we just took the shuttle from there to the school this morning. Couldn't we have slept in and met Mr. Jeddee here? Anyway, he wants us to take a look at what's going on in one of the laboratories. I don't know many people

on the station yet. Unfortunately, it turns out I'm pretty familiar with the scientist in charge of this particular lab.

Aww, man. Of all the scientists in all the laboratories on this whole space station, it would be just my luck to end up with my dad. And his "jokes." I won't live this down anytime soon.

Oh, and look—it gets even better. He has Bula with him. Super. Don't know why she's not in her preschool class. It must be Bring a Whiny Pest to Work Day.

"Follow me," says Dad. "Our lab is at the end of the corridor."

"Well, here we are!" says Dad as we reach the end of the corridor. Two metal doors slide apart with a swoosh, and we all step inside.

Whoa! This is the most humongous laboratory I've ever seen! I've been to all the ones Mom and Dad worked in back home, and none of those were even close. And I've watched Dad work on hundreds of robots before, but nothing like these. That one by the platform must be at least a hundred feet tall!

Rand-El taps me on the shoulder. "Wow!" he says. "Your dad made those?!"

"Pretty much. He designed them and sent the

plans through the wormhole months ago. They were assembled before we got here."

"Wow! It must be a blast living with your family! My dad's area of expertise is soil. You know . . . dirt."

"Dirt, eh?" says Dad. He must have overheard us. "I can dig it. HAR!"

Rand-El leans toward me. "And he's hilarious, too!"

Hilarious? That word must have a different meaning on Rand-El's planet. Like "not funny."

 "Does anyone have any questions before we get started?"

"This place is huge! Are you the only scientist in here?"

 "Only one? Heck, I'm not even the only Professor Klosmo here."

"You mean you have a clone?!"

"No. A wife. And she probably thinks one of me running around here is plenty."

"Actually, it's one too many."

"HAR! This is the other Professor Klosmo. She's a neuroscientist. She works with brains. We share this lab because we're working on a project together."

They go on to explain how they're attempting to put people's minds into robotic bodies. They even demonstrate how the mind-transfer beam works.

"So there you have it. Are there any more questions?"

"Yeah. What happens to the person's body once the mind is out of it and in the robot?"

"Well, not all of the mind actually transfers into the robot. A tiny portion remains in the brain. Not enough to think, but just enough to perform basic functions like moving around and eating and going to the bathroom. Sort of like Grandpa Karl, eh, Kelvin? HAR!"

"Or Bula."

"Speaking of Bula . . . where is she?"

"I thought you had her."

"I thought you had her!"

"Bula!" Mom screams. "How did you get up there?"

"She must have gone up the elevator and crawled across the catwalk," Dad says. "Keep her busy. I'll go and get her."

Apparently, the elevator can only be controlled with the buttons inside the elevator car. And it's stuck at the top, where Bula left it. So Dad starts to climb up the framework as my classmates look on in awe. About halfway up, Dad's foot slips off the cross brace and he's flailing for something to hold on to. The kids gasp. Mom screams.

WHOOPSIE! LOOKS LIKE WE WERE ALMOST DOWN TO ONE PROFESSOR KLOSMO. HAR!!

The kids all laugh. Dad makes his way to the top, grabs Bula, and brings her down the elevator. When they reach the bottom, Mom runs over to hug Bula, while my whole class cheers wildly. This field trip turned out way better than I expected!

 "So, were you worried about me up there?"

"Not a bit. I had my finger over the Gravity Off button the whole time."

"Really? That's cheating!"

"Hey, I didn't want you falling on your head—your jokes might get even worse. The kids loved your bravery, anyway. It's just a shame we can't tell them the truth about what we're doing here."

"I hear you, but that's sort of the point of a top secret project. Besides, the last thing a bunch of twelve-year-olds need to worry about is their universe being destroyed by a super energy orb."

"Well, I still feel bad about lying."

"I wouldn't call it lying, exactly. We really are putting living minds into robots. Just not quite for the reasons we said. And unless somebody finds a way to prevent flesh-and-blood beings from turning to goo when they get anywhere near that Zorb, our project is the only chance we've got."

"What about the remote-controlled robot experiments they're conducting over in laboratory six? Hasn't that group made any progress?"

"Nope. The Zorb's energy jams the signal whenever one of the robots gets close."

"Then it looks like it's all up to us. The sooner we recover the Zorb and secure it in that containment chamber, the better I'll feel. I can't even imagine what might happen if it fell into the wrong hands."

OH, BUT I CAN!

So that's what they're up to! I knew there had to be more going on. A superpowerful energy source capable of destroying the entire universe? Now, that is something that Erik Failenheimer must possess! And possess it Erik Failenheimer shall!

I will transfer my own brilliant mind in to the body of that enormous robot. YES! Let those clodhopping Klosmos do all the research and all the work. I, Erik Failenheimer, will reap the benefit! I, Erik Failenheimer, will receive the final glory!

And now, with a simple pull of this lever, I will finally have the spectacular body my brilliant brain so richly deserves! BWAHAHAHAHA!!!

But wait. Perhaps I shouldn't rush into this. Perhaps I should be patient and find out more about this orb and its true capabilities. Perhaps I should take the time to thoroughly read through the mind-transfer beam's instruction manual before I use it on myself.

Nah.

ord of Dad rescuing Bula from the robot head is spreading through the hallways like the smell of the boiled glootnip the cafeteria served today. So is talk about how "hilarious" he is. That's right. My dad and "hilarious" in the same sentence—without the word "not." Either (a) I've been misjudging him all these years, or (b) the rest of the universe has a terrible sense of humour.

"Hey, Kelvin. What happens when you give a splornax a bowl of gloot-nip?"

"Uh . . . I don't know."

"Me either, but I sure wouldn't want to find out! HAR!"

Uh . . . yeah. I'm pretty sure it's (b). And did he just say "HAR"? Please tell me he did not just say "HAR."

On the bright side, it looks like I won't have to spend the rest of my time here being embarrassed by my parents. The kids at school seem to think they're actually pretty cool. Kinda makes me wonder what their parents must be like.

I feel a tap on my shoulder. It's Zot.

 "That was pretty awesome this afternoon. The field trip, I mean."

"Yeah. I guess you don't see something like that every day."

 "Hardly ever! It must be neat to live with such cool parents."

See what I mean?

"Anyway, I was wondering if maybe you wanted to get together after school and go over the . . ."

Hey, that's her—the girl from my geography class! Boy, I didn't have any girls like her in my schools back on Earth. Well, Wendy Trasnik was pretty cute. But she didn't glow. This girl actually seems to glow. Her eyes are different colours, too. And I don't mean from each other. Each one is made up of a bunch of different colours, kind of like that kaleidoscope I had when I was little. And those teeth! They're as perfect and white as . . .

What? Oh no. Please tell me Luna didn't hear that.

No, no, no, no, no! This can't be happening! "Who is this Neanderthal, anyway?" I ask Spotch.

"Oh, that's Dorn," he says. "Biggest bully in the school. In fact, he's pretty much the only bully in the school. And the kid with him is Teddy, but everybody calls him Backpack. I think Dorn's mom is the head of security for the whole space station. I'll tell you one thing—you do not want to get on his bad side."

"Does he have any other kind?" I say. "What's he got against me, anyway?"

"Who knows," says Spotch. "Maybe you remind him of his parole officer."

Dorn comes over and takes my helmet down off my locker.

 "Nice helmet. Do you fit into it?"

"Well ... uh ... I ..."

 "Let's see."

THWUSH!

KLUNK!

 "Hey! I guess so! Now let's see if you're smart enough to get out. Ha!"

I'll say this for my new school—it's not dull. Painful sometimes, but not dull. And now I'm starving.

"Did you learn anything today?" Mom asks.

"I guess so." I actually learned four things today:

1. My whole body can fit into a space designed only for my head if enough force is applied.
2. It takes two people thirteen minutes to pull me back out again.
3. When you're thirteen minutes late for gym class, Coach Ed makes you run ten laps around the gymnasium wearing triple-gravity boots.
4. I hate triple-gravity boots.

All of which led to my current starvation situation.

"I'm really hungry, Dad. What's for dinner?"

"Synthesized hot dogs! And I must say, they look delicious!"

Of course they look delicious. The food synthesizers in our LIV-space kitchens do a great job of, as the brochure says, "re-creating the look of your home planet's most popular dishes."

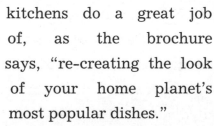
DING!

And I guess that's true. I mean, it looks like you're eating a hot dog. It feels like you're eating a hot dog. But it tastes like you're eating a hot-dog-shaped tube of pencil erasers. Which is probably why Bula likes them so much. It's also why it's strange that she's bawling her eyes out, since this is her favourite meal.

"What's wrong with Bula?" I ask. "I mean besides all the obvious stuff."

"She can't find Fluffles," Mom says. Dad shakes his head. "We've turned this place over looking for him. It's like he just got up and walked away."

Bula's crying gets worse the more we talk about it. All this whining is getting on my last nerve. I kind of wish I had climbed up that robot today before anyone knew she was in there and locked the dome. After all, it's probably sound-proof. Hey . . . wait a minute!

I look at Dad. "Did she have Fluffles when you pulled her out of the robot this afternoon?"

"I'm not sure. I don't think so." Dad's getting excited now. "Hurry up and finish eating, and

127

we'll go down to the lab and take a look!"

After dinner Dad, Bula, and I head down to the lab. She's stopped bawling, but now snot is hanging out of both nostrils. When she breathes in, it gets sucked back up into her nose. Then she breathes out and it dangles down again. Over and over like two slimy yo-yos. Man, little sisters are gross.

We enter the lab, and as we head for the lift, we see something on the ground near the robot's foot.

It's Fluffles. Yikes! It looks like he fell into a blender or something. Dad picks him up. "What the heck happened to you, fella?" he says as he hands Bula the plushy. As soon as she gets a good look at it, she of course starts bawling again. Even worse than before.

Dad takes Fluffles from Bula and heads over to his workbench. "Don't worry, sweetie. We'll clean him up, fix him up, and make him even better than he was before." Really, Dad? You've got some industrial-strength snot remover in your toolbox?

A few moments earlier . . .

Ugh . . . what happened? . . . why am I in the dark? . . . And why do I feel like I was hit by a bus . . . and fell over a cliff . . . and landed in a truck full of broken glass . . . that then blew up?

Wait! The mind-transfer beam! Now I remember. I wonder if it worked. It's so dark that I can't see anything. I wonder if my eyes are open. I wonder if I even have eyes to open.

There! My vision is returning!

There I am, down below! Which means my mind is up here in the robot! YES! It worked! The brilliant mind of Erik Failenheimer now resides within one of the most powerful robots in the galaxy! Who would dare challenge me?! BWAHAHAHAHA!!!

I think I'll take my new body out for a spin. Just a step to begin with.

It feels like I took a step. A really little one. But the robot didn't move. This might

take some getting used to. Let's try flapping
the arms.

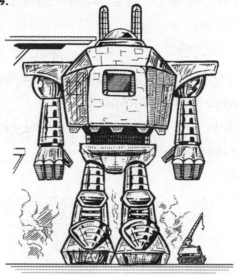

Hmm. Maybe if I try bending over and
touching my toes.

What is this?! I'm not hard and cold and metallic—I'm soft and warm and fuzzy!

Zarfloots!! I look like a chewed-up dog toy! Oh, this is just great. I'll really strike fear into the masses now. And how do I even get down? Maybe there is something on the robot that I could . . .

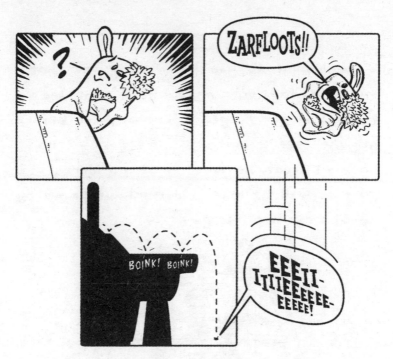

NOOOOO! Drat these slippery, fuzzy feet! From ruler of the universe to a lifeless splat on some laboratory floor in deep space. Life just isn't fair.

Hey! What do you know? I guess that's one advantage over my old body. Wait! My old body! I've got to get it out of here before anyone sees it. But . . . it's gone! I must have—I mean he must have wandered off. Just as well. At least I don't have to worry about anyone finding—

Zarfloots! Someone is coming! I better play dead.

I hear voices. It sounds like they're coming this way! Please just keep on walking. Please don't . . .

. . . pick me up. Oh, wonderful! As if I haven't been humiliated enough today, now I'm being manhandled by that insipid scientist. It's okay, Erik. Just stay calm and motionless. You've made it this far. It can't get any worse.

seriously?! why couldn't that fall just have killed me? what's going on now? where is klosmo taking me? It's a bench. I guess this isn't so terrible. Nothing bad ever happened to anybody lying on a bench.

Are you kidding me? How about you just throw me into a pit of starving alligators? maybe run over me a few times with a lawn mower. slather me with honey and toss me to a bear cub.

Hey, now! This turned out way better than I expected. I actually look rather handsome, if I do say so myself. Maybe this won't be so bad after all.

DAY 3

What a morning. I woke up late, so I had to skip my synthesized scrambled-eggs-and-bacon breakfast. Not that I really minded—they taste pretty much like the synthesized hot dogs. And the synthesized pizza. And the synthesized lemonade. The real issue was not having enough time to gel my hair after my daily run-in with the Vacuu-Suk 3000. I spend most of Ms. Gassias's first-hour maths class using the old saliva-in-the-hand method to get it to lie down. My success level is not high.

When first hour ends, I meet up with Spotch on our way to Professor Plutz's galactic geography class.

"Whoa, Kelv. What did you do—stick half your head in a shuttle engine?"

I haven't known Spotch for long, but I'm getting the feeling he speaks his mind. No sugar-coating with old Spotcho.

 "Nah, I didn't have time to use any hair gel this morning. Hey, you wouldn't have any on you, would you?"

"Nope. I have some antenna gel, but it would probably just

**make your hair fall out. Which,
come to think of it, might be an
improvement."**

Now, that may be Spotch's idea of a joke or just a factual statement. It's hard to tell sometimes.

We make our way into the classroom and grab the last two open desks, way in the back. My chair has a backpack sitting in it. A blue tentacle reaches across from the next desk over and snatches the backpack.

"Sorry about that, Kelvin," the tentacle's owner says. He has three other tentacles, too, but they're all busy at the moment, writing and turning notebook pages and scratching what I guess must be his nose.

"Didn't know you wanted to sit here, pal," Tentacles continues. "Hey, maybe we could be homework buddies, huh? I'd even let you do most of the work! I know you smart guys like to do most of the work! What do you say?"

"I'll think about it," I answer, knowing full

well I won't. It's amazing how popular a genius becomes when homework is due.

Professor Plutz calls Gil up to the front of the classroom and activates a holographic map of the galaxy.

"Mr. Lagoonie. Please point out to the class where our fine school is located within the Milky Way galaxy."

Poor Gil. He clearly has no idea where we are on that map, and he's starting to panic. I can't watch anymore, so I let my eyes wander. And they just happen to wander a couple rows over.

 "So, what's up with Luna?"

"Luna? Let me guess. You think she's cute."

 "Well . . . yeah. I mean, she is pretty awesome. She almost seems to have a glow about her."

"She does have a glow about her. Everybody from her planet does. Something about bioluminescence."

Gil looks like he's really sweating it out up there, although it's hard to tell, since he's in a water-filled sphere. He's pointing all over the place on the map, and Professor Plutz keeps shaking his head no. It's as if Gil is continually pushing the head-shake button on a Professor Plutz remote control. I sure am glad it's not me up there.

 "You may take your seat, Mr. Lagoonie. Mr. Klosmo, why don't you give it a try."

What? Yikes! I don't know anything about galactic geography. And I definitely have no idea where we are on that map. The only reason I even know it's the Milky Way is because Plutz said it is. Gil is going to look like Copernicus navigating that thing compared with me.

I've seen it happen a lot at other schools. A new kid shows up and gets labeled by the other kids right away. And it usually sticks. If he's lucky, it will be something like the cool kid. Or the funny kid. Or the smart kid. If he's not so lucky, it could be the weirdo. Or the dummy. Or the slob. And once you get a label, it's really tough to get rid of.

I was lucky. I arrived with a reputation of being a genius right off the bat. But it's one thing to be called a genius because you actually are one. It's another thing altogether if it's because you're the exact opposite—if it's because the kids think you're actually a doofus. It's like calling a short kid Paul Bunyan. Or a slow kid Speedy Gonzales. Sarcasm is big in junior high. As of right now I'm still the smart genius to these guys. But the way things are going, it won't be long before I'm the other one. And then who will want to hang out with me?

I get up and head toward the front of the class. Slowly. As in two-inch steps. Maybe if I take long enough, my Mighty Mega Supergeniusness will kick in by the time I get up there. Or maybe the bell will ring.

It's no use. Everybody is staring at me. Luna is looking at me like I've got a porcupine stapled to my head. I make my way to the map, at regular speed, and prepare to begin my life as a doofus genius. Mom and Dad will be so proud.

 "I must say, Mr. Klosmo, that it certainly is an honour to have you in our class! There aren't many teachers who can say they've had the pleasure of teaching the smartest student in the galaxy."

Here we go again. . . .

 "This must seem like such a simple question for you. Perhaps we could make it a bit more challenging by having you close your eyes first?"

Oh, sure. Why the heck not? Maybe I could stand on my head and juggle penguins with my feet at the same time, too. It's not like any of that is going to make a difference. The jig is up. Nothing can save me from embarrassing myself this time—

What the heck is that?" I yell to Spotch over the noise.

"Fire drill," he says. Fire drill? Awesome! It looks like my secret is safe, at least for another hour. "Or maybe an actual fire," he adds. "Who knows?"

A real fire? That could be bad. I could be seriously hurt. I could even die. We all could. But to be honest, the whole secret-being-safe thing has me pretty pumped right now.

"Okay," Professor Plutz shouts to the class. "You

know the drill. Exit the classroom calmly and in single file, and head straight to your lockers. And keep your hands to yourselves. I'm looking at you, Marvin!"

I've never been through a fire drill in space before, so I stick close to Spotch as we head to our lockers. Once we get there, we put on our helmets, and Spotch attaches a cable hanging from his locker to his belt.

 "What the heck is this thing for?"

"Attach it to your belt, so when they open the air lock, you're not sucked out into space."

 "Oh."

"If there's a real fire, they'll open the nearest air lock and suck out all the oxygen until the fire goes out. That's why we have to wear our helmets and strap in."

 "Do you think this is a real fire?"

"If it is, we're going to need a new principal."

Spotch points behind me. A helmetless

Principal Ort is slithering down the hallway toward us.

"You were all too slow getting secured to your lockers. TOO slow! DANGEROUSLY slow! I-OBVIOUSLY-DON'T-CARE-IF-I-GET-SUCKED-OUT-INTO-SPACE-OR-BURNED-TO-A-CRISP slow! If this were an actual fire, there is no telling how many of you would be floating around outside the school right now. We need to improve on this.

"Also, this was most definitely NOT a scheduled fire drill. Someone pulled the alarm. And when I find out who the culprit is, he or she will be in big trouble. BIG trouble! MAJOR trouble! YOU-DON'T-EVEN-WANT-TO-THINK-ABOUT-IT trouble!"

Ort slithers back down the corridor, leaving a trail of slime behind. So, no real fire. That's a relief. Plus, we got to leave class before I had to answer that question, so at least I didn't look like a doofus in front of everybody.

Until now, that is.

On the bright side, it took Spotch and Mippitt only nine minutes to pull me out of my helmet this time. Of course, that still made me late for lunch. Which also made me late for science class after lunch. Fortunately, Mr. Jeddee doesn't have triple-gravity boots to punish me with, so I just walk in and sit down at my group table. Mr. Jeddee doesn't even acknowledge the fact that I'm late. I have a feeling somebody told him what happened.

 "What's wrong with Grimnee?"

"She heard about what Dorn did to you. Grimnee doesn't like bullies."

 "Who does?"

"No. I mean Grimnee really doesn't like bullies. She got teased a lot back on her home planet for being so skinny."

159

"So . . . skinny?"

 "Yeah. Remember, on her planet the gravity is so high that everybody has to be pretty thick and muscular just to move around."

 "It also means she doesn't know her own strength in the lighter gravity we have out here."

Note to self—never make fun of anyone around Grimnee.

"I have graded your short science essays from last week. Overall, I am quite pleased, although some of you need to show a bit more consistency in your work."

Mr. Jeddee hands the papers back. I wasn't here last week, so I didn't have to write one. And the way things are going, that's probably just as well. Everyone in the group looks pretty pleased with their grades . . . except Brian. "What's up?" I ask. "Didn't do as well as you thought?" He hands me his paper.

LIGHT SPEED
Brian Stem
Mr. Jeddee
3rd hour

When taking into consideration that the speed of light, or c, is approximately 186,282 miles per second (299,792 kilometres per second), it becomes apparent that the light we see emanating from distant stars is, in actuality, hundreds or even thousands of years old. This, in turn, means that we are seeing the star as it appeared hundreds or thousands of years ago.

Which is awesome when you think about it. I mean, the star you see up in the sky might not even **BE** there anymore! It could have exploded or collapsed or something since the light we see left the star. How cool is that?

I LiKe PuddinG.

 "Also, I am handing out your group science projects today. I'm sure you all remember the large robot we saw during our field trip yesterday."

"Huh? Robot? Field trip?"

"Each group will be assigned a system on the robot, such as navigation or communication. You will write a detailed overview of that system and present it to the class."

Mr. Jeddee walks around the room, handing out the project assignments. Our group gets propulsion. Rand-El taps me on the shoulder. "Hey, Kelvin. I know you're a genius and all, and you probably want to do this whole thing yourself to get a good grade, but can you let the rest of us do our share, too? I'm actually really interested in propulsion systems. In fact, that's why I started the rocket club."

"Oh . . . absolutely!" I tell him. I don't tell him he can feel free to do my share, too. But he can. "In fact, you guys can take the lead and do most of the work. I can just sort of look things over as we go, if you want. You know, to make sure you're doing it right." Man, this is a perfect setup. I was born to be a supervisor.

"Actually, you can do more than that. The robot is in your mom and dad's lab, right?"

I don't know if I like where Rand-El is going with this.

"Maybe you could sneak us all in one night to get a good look at that robot when nobody is around."

Yup. There it is.

"Yeah! Come on, Kelvin," the rest of the gang joins in. Except Mippitt. He never talks.

"Well . . . uh . . . I don't know," I tell them. "How am I supposed to get us in there?"

Rand-El looks at me like I'm nuts. "How? Come on, Kelvin. You'll figure something out. I mean, you *are* the smartest kid in the galaxy. Right?"

"Well, this was certainly a wonderful way to waste the entire evening. I don't know how you put up with it day after day, Mr. Nosebutton. By the way—why did she give you such a ridiculous name?"

"Oh. I see. Bah. None of this matters anyway. Very soon these silly tea party games will be a thing of the past, and I, Erik Failenheimer, will RULE THE UNIVERSE! BWAHAHAHAHA!!! What do you think of that, Miss Hairzybearzy?"

"Not impressed, I see. Well, I'll have you know that I have devised a new plan to steal the ultrapowerful Zorb, since my original plan to transfer my brilliant mind into the body of a robot hit a few snags."

"You find that amusing do you, Mrs. Fuzzface? It's not a big deal, really. I don't even need my mind in the robot. You see, although no living being can go anywhere near that Zorb without turning into a puddle of goo,

my new body has no such restric-
tions!"

"Don't look so surprised, Mr. Nosebutton. There are a few advantages
to being made of cotton and polyester. And taking the Zorb from that
secret planetoid is one of them."

"What's that, Miss Hairzybearzy? If it's a secret planetoid, how will I find it? No need to worry. I have a plan for that as well. And I intend to get started on it immediately. But first . . ."

Ah, now that felt good! It turns out this being-evil thing is right up my alley. I should have thought of it years ago. And this little tea party turmoil is just a small sampling of what I have in store for the rest of this pathetic universe! But first I need the key card to Klosmo's lab so I can hack into his computer. I saw him put it down on the table by the front door.

DAY 4

176

Ugh. I can hardly keep my eyes open. I guess that's what happens when you stay up half the night trying to figure out a way to sneak seven classmates into your parents' top secret laboratory. Especially when one of them sloshes around in a giant goldfish bowl. And the worst part is what I came up with—which is nothing. Zip. Zippo. Zilch. Nada. Well, unless you count synonyms for "nothing."

I walk into Ms. Gassias's maths class. She's not here yet. Good. Maybe I can catch a minute or two of shut-eye. Then again, maybe not. Luna is sitting in the middle of the classroom, and there's a seat open right behind her. Here's my opportunity! I quickly make my way over to the open desk.

SLOOSH!

What is it with this guy? What did I ever do to him? Well, the seat next to him is open. I guess I'll just take that one and hope he doesn't decide to cram me into my backpack.

 "Sorry again, brainiac, but that's my right foot's seat."

Dorn puts his foot on the desk. I see that the desk next to him on the other side is open. I may not be a Mighty Mega Supergenius—yet—but I'm smart enough to know where this is going.

"Let me guess—you're using that desk, too, right?"

"Nope."

"Really? I . . . uh . . . I guess I'll just sit over there, then."

"But my left foot is."

Wow. Dorn may be a jerk, but I've got to give him credit for being flexible. Although I doubt he can fit his whole body into a helmet, like I can. Anyway, there's another seat open in the back, next to Rand-El. I sit down without a hitch. Dorn is eyeballing me, but apparently, he isn't quite that flexible.

As I'm taking my book out of my backpack, I hear a deep, growling sound from the other side of the room. It's getting louder. It's Grimnee, and she's clomping her way toward the centre of the room. She doesn't look happy.

Yikes! Zot wasn't kidding. Grimnee really doesn't like bullies! She rolls Dorn out into the hallway, closes the door, and sits back down. Her desktop is missing a large, hand-shaped chunk.

Rand-El leans over. "So, Kelvin, how are we going to get into that lab?"

Gee, I thought he'd never ask. "I don't know yet," I tell him. "We need to use one of my parents' key cards, but if they find out I took it, I'll be toast."

Rand-El looks disappointed. "I already talked to the rest of the group, and they all think they can sneak out of their LIV spaces tonight. This might be the only time everybody can make it."

"Well, my parents are going to Bula's art fair tonight, and they'll have their key cards with them. But I'll see what I can do. By the way, why do you sit way back here? I can hardly see the screen."

"Not a problem," Rand-El says. "My top set of eyes is great for long distances. I can read a text-book from five hundred feet away."

I'm confused. "Then why do you wear glasses?"

"Because," he says, "they look cool. The top ones don't even have lenses in them."

Ms. Gassias enters the room.

She's a cloud of gas, although she won't tell us what kind. I can tell you this much, though—she's definitely not odourless.

"Kelvin, would you do us the honour of coming up and solving today's first problem? I'm sure this all seems too simple for a young man of your cognitive abilities, but it would help the rest of the class to see it done correctly."

Man, I cannot catch a break at this school! I was able to do most of the homework, but Ms. Gassias always puts the hardest problems up on the screen. And they're usually *waaay* over my head.

"Oh, I wouldn't want to hog the best problems, Ms. Gassias. Why don't you go ahead and let somebody else give it a try."

"Nonsense, Mr. Klosmo. Stop being so modest and come on up here. I'm hoping to learn something myself."

All right. Here goes nothing. I can't see the screen from back here. Maybe it's not too tough of a problem after all. Maybe I'll luck out and I can fudge my way through it. I get up and slowly walk to the front of the class. As I get closer, the screen comes into focus.

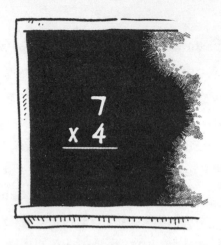

Wait! I know this one! I can do this! Prepare to be impressed, Luna. Ol' Kelvin is going to strut his stuff. I grab the stylus and begin to write, pausing a couple times to stroke my chin so everybody thinks I'm a real thinker.

Wait a minute. Why is everyone laughing? Oh no—please don't tell me I got it wrong. I'm positive that's right! Well, almost positive.

"**Funny as well as brilliant, I see, Mr. Klosmo. That problem, of course, was left on the screen from some tutoring I was doing with a third grader this morning. Here is your problem.**"

$$3x^3 + 2xy - 4y = 89$$

$$\begin{array}{r} 7 \\ \times\ 4 \\ \hline 28 \end{array}$$

$$x =$$

$$y =$$

Yikes! Is that a maths problem or a secret launch code? I don't hear any fire alarms going off, either, so I'm toast for sure this time. Maybe I can talk Mom and Dad into homeschooling me so I never have to come out of my room again.

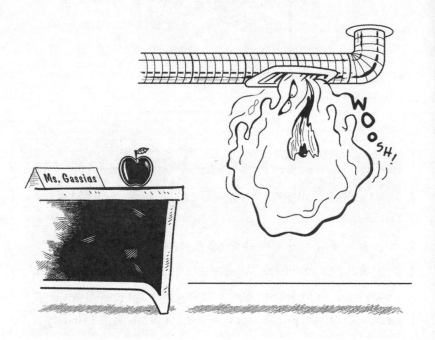

Or not. Okay, this is getting weird.

Drat! I can't see a thing. I just hope Klosmo is going straight to his laboratory and not dillydallying around. I have secrets to uncover!

I hear a door opening. Wait.

We've stopped and he's set the briefcase down. I can hear workers grunting. And that sounds like propulsion fluid swishing through pipes and into the robots' fuel tanks. We must be in the laboratory!

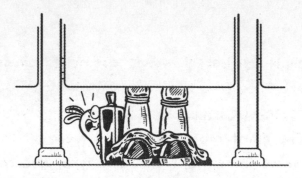

Zarfloots! At least the glue has clogged my nostrils.

20 minutes later . . .

We're moving again. Well, it's about time! I was beginning to think that bespectacled blockhead had fallen asleep. We're making our way down a long corridor and through another door. Klosmo is setting the briefcase down again and walking away.

I'm almost afraid to look.

Well, that's better. Now I just need to access the Zorb files, find the planetoid's location, hide until everyone leaves for the evening, climb up into the giant robot's control dome, pilot it to that same planetoid, locate the Zorb, and take it for myself. Easy peasy!

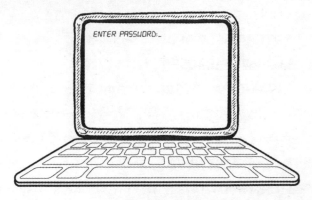

ENTER PASSWORD:_

Zarfloots! I forgot about the password. Well, how hard could it be to figure out? I just need to put myself in Klosmo's head, to think like he would think.

ENTER PASSWORD:
IAMSTUPID
INVALID PASSWORD. TRY AGAIN.

Double zarfloots! This may take a while.

ENTER PASSWORD:
IAMALOSER
INVALID PASSWORD. TRY AGAIN.

ENTER PASSWORD:
IAMASTUPIDLOSER
INVALID PASSWORD. TRY AGAIN.

ENTER PASSWORD:
EVERYBODYHATESME
INVALID PASSWORD. TRY AGAIN.

Okay, this is going nowhere fast. My own thoughts about that sad-sack scientist keep getting in the way. I may as well let a monkey type in passwords at this point. But it's not my fault. It's hard to concentrate when I can overhear Klosmo telling all those

pathetic jokes to his assistants. How can
they get any work done with such lame . . .
WAIT! I'VE GOT IT!

ENTER PASSWORD:
HAR!
CORRECT PASSWORD.

I can't believe that wasn't my first guess.
Not that it matters—I'm in the system! Now
to access the Zorb data!

Ah, so that's why it's called the Zorb. Although they could have named it the Ploopy-dooper, for all I care. Now that I have the coordinates, all that remains is to hide until the laboratory empties, and the universe is as good as mine. ZOUNDS! If I weren't 70 percent polyester, I'd be getting goose bumps right now!

In fact, I'm in such a wonderfully EVIL mood that, before I hide, I simply MUST get my revenge on that cretin Klosmo! I must make him suffer like he made me suffer for all those years. I must do something so awful, so heinous, so diabolically EVIL, that he will NEVER recover!

CLICK!
CLICK!

BWAHAHAHAHA!!!

Uh-oh. Someone's coming! Time to play dead again. Who would give a second glance at a stuffed rabbit lying on a desk?

I'm starting to LOVE Coach Ed's gym class, even though he made me run laps for being late the other day. And it sure has nothing to do with being a great athlete, because I'm not. A great athlete, I mean. When your parents are the smartest scientists on your entire planet, you can't really expect to inherit a ton of athletic ability from them.

And I didn't.

The closest thing they have to a sports-related skill is bowling, and that's only if you can call a 57 average "skill." That's my mom, by the way. My dad's average is 42. To put that in perspective, a friend back at one of my old Earth schools told me that an orangutan once bowled a 127. That's right—an ape is a better bowler than both my parents combined. I'd hate to see what a chimpanzee could do.

The reason I like gym is there's no pressure on me to be a genius. Coach Ed isn't parading me up in front of the class to show off my brilliance at throwing a ball or jumping over a hurdle. Coach Ed isn't even alive. He's a SportBot, and a pretty old one, at that. PhysEd-201 is his official designation, and apparently, he used to be a galaxy-class glormball player. But he's seen better days.

And that's Tor in the airchair. He's Coach Ed's student assistant and by far the biggest sports fan in the school. He knows who holds every record in every sport on every planet in the galaxy. Unfortunately, he can't tell you what he had for breakfast yesterday because every memory cell is being used to store sports data. And even though he has six legs, they're too weak to support his weight, so Tor can't play any of the sports himself.

 "Listen up, everybody. Today we're going to learn the proper technique for hitting a glorm with a fleenor racket. Now, I don't mean to brag, but back at the Kragwin Championships of '83, I splorted the winning goal with one second left in the final period, giving my team the Division 22 Intergalactic League title. So I know what I'm talking about."

I'm glad someone does.

"The key to a successful splort is in the follow-through. Now watch closely."

 "Okay—any questions?"

"Yeah, is your arm supposed to go farther than the glorm?"

"Only after years of practice. Now, I need a couple volunteers."

See? He didn't ask for me specifically to demonstrate in front of the class. I'm just another student to Coach Ed. Nothing special. And I like it that way.

"I'll do it."

 "Very good. And who else would like to give it a try?"

"Hey, how about the genius? Unwess he's afwaaaaaaid."

Oh, c'mon! So much for this being my favourite class.

 "Um . . . I would, but I have a bit of an upset stomach from lunch. I should

198

probably just sit over here until it settles down."

"What's the matter, smart guy? Grimnee's not here to save your sorry behind? What a putz."

 "I'll do it!"

What? Zot? Play glormball against Dorn? No way this ends well. Dorn is as much a gentleman as a cow is a video game player. I mean, what with the hooves and all. He's going to massacre her. He'll massacre me, too, but I can't let Zot take the hit.

 "It's okay, Coach Ed. I'll do it."

"Like heck you will! Sit that upset stomach of yours down, Kelv. No one wants to see what you had for lunch."

Whoa! I don't know anything about glormball, but that was impressive!

"Hey, everybody! I'm home! And boy, oh boy, does something smell terrific!"

That "something" would be the synthesized mac and cheese Mom made for dinner. It tastes just like the hot dogs. I've tried drowning it in synthesized salt, but that doesn't work because the salt tastes just like the mac and cheese. And the hot dogs. And the sofa cushions. I actually look forward to eating in the cafeteria at school, because they don't use synthesizers. Sure, the food from other parts of the galaxy can be a bit . . . different . . .

. . . but at least it's real. In fact, sometimes it's so real it crawls down my throat all by itself.

But back to Dad's comment. "Really?" I say. "This stuff doesn't even have a smell. Or a taste."

Dad rubs his hands together excitedly. "I know. It reminds me of our dinners back on Earth. HAR!"

"But before we eat, I have a couple surprises." Dad opens up his briefcase and pulls Fluffles out.

He looks angrier than I remember. "I found this little fella down in the lab. I have no idea how he got there. Maybe he hitched a ride on my briefcase this morning! HAR!"

Bula runs over and snatches the plushy. "Fluf-flee Mufflee! I've been looking for you all day!" she squeals. "C'mon, let's go in my room. I have a big surprise for you!"

Dad is still at the door, his goofy grin goofier than usual.

 "I thought you said you had a couple of surprises."

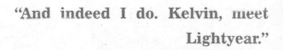 "And indeed I do. Kelvin, meet Lightyear."

"He belonged to one of the other scientists, but he kept getting into stuff in the laboratory, so he had to go. I figured, hey, we could use a pet! So . . . voilà!"

 "Hey, I remember him. He was in one of the rooms we passed on our field trip to your lab. So you mean he's ours? To keep?"

"Sure is—as long as we take good care of him. Watch out, though. I hear he'll eat just about anything. Well, except for your mom's cooking. HAR!"

Wow. Dad's in rare form. Who cares, though, because THIS is awesome! Our very own dog! Or whatever the heck he is.

 "Is it okay if I play with Lightyear in my room for a bit?"

"I suppose so. Make it quick, though. We're eating in ten minutes."

We head back to my room and I close the door. I really want to see what this little guy can do. Who knows? Maybe he's a lot smarter than an Earth dog.

"Okay, Lightyear," I say. "Sit."

"Shake hands."

"Lie down."

PANT!
PANT!

So I guess that's a no on the whole smart thing. He does look like he's having fun, though. I wonder if he's a retriever? I grab the rubber ball that's sitting on my desk. "You want to play ball, boy?" Lightyear snaps to attention, his tongue and tail both wagging furiously. I toss the ball across the room, and Lightyear immediately pounces into action. He scoops it up, races back over to where I'm sitting on the floor, and drops the ball. Now that's more like it.

And then I get the biggest, wettest face lick of my life. My glasses are covered in so much slobber I can't see. "Really, Lightyear?" I say as I remove the glasses to clean off the drool. Lightyear stares at me for a second and then . . . eats the rubber ball. And I don't mean he bites it or chews on it. He eats the whole thing—just scarfs it down in one big gulp. And then things really start getting weird.

I call Spotch and Rand-El and tell them to get over here right now.

A short time earlier . . .

This is unacceptable! I've been trapped in this infernal briefcase for what seems like days . . . squashed on top of a half-eaten cheese and onion sandwich. The only upside is I can't hear Klosmo's terrible jokes. Except, of course, for the "HARS." Those come through loud and clear. When I rule the universe, "HARS" will be punishable by death.

My patience is wearing thin. The universe rightfully belongs to ME and I want to rule it NOW! If I must wait even another minute, I will surely—hold on! What's this?! We're moving!

Klosmo must be moving the briefcase to another part of the lab. When he opens it up, I simply need to "accidentally" fall out and roll under a table or something before I'm spotted.

I can hear the sound of lift doors opening. And now closing. We're moving upward. We must be heading to the robot's control dome. Excellent! This might work out even better than I hoped for. Now we're moving forward again. I don't remember it being this long of a walk.

Klosmo is setting the briefcase down. I can hear the locks being fumbled with. Here's my chance!

Oh, for the love of biscuits, not again! I really thought I'd seen the last of that ponytailed pipsqueak. Honestly, how can one infernal family bring one cuddly, fuzzy little evil scientist so much anguish?

I would have to say, without a doubt,
that this is the low point of my career.

until now.

I quickly wolf down my dinner and am back in my room with Lightyear when Rand-El and Spotch arrive. Spotch seems a little put out.

"What's so important that we had to rush over here? I didn't even get to finish my dessert."

"GET to finish your dessert? Wait, you actually like the synthesized food?"

"Sure. It's just like what we have back home. These synthesizers are awesome."

"But there's no flavour."

"What's flavour?"

I make a mental note to cross Spotch's home planet off my list of future vacation destinations. I sense a bit of impatience from the two of them, so I make my reveal of Lightyear, who I had hiding under the desk.

"Whoa. What the hcck is that?"

"THAT is Lightyear. He's our new pet. Well, sort of, anyway."

"He's sort of yours?"

"No, he's all ours. He's sort of a

pet. My dad brought him home
from the lab today. But that's not
the best part!"

HE THREW UP AND *THESE* CAME OUT.

 "He ate your spare glasses and
horked them up again? That's gross,
Kelvin."

"No, he ate a ball and threw them
up. And I don't even have spare
glasses."

"So he ate someone else's glasses and horked them back up again. You can't really blame him. I'd have an upset stomach, too, if I swallowed a ball and a pair of glasses."

"No, he threw up an exact copy of my glasses! Made of the same rubber as the ball!"

"Impossible. He could have got ahold of those glasses anywhere. They're a fairly common style, after all."

"Oh yeah? Well, how about Rand-El's glasses? They're pretty unique, wouldn't you say?"

"Not on my planet, they aren't. But out here most of you guys only have two or three eyes, so yeah."

"Okay, now take them off and hold them in front of Lightyear."

Rand-El obviously isn't too keen about this, but he does it anyway. I unscrew the lightbulb from my desk lamp and give it to Lightyear, who immediately inhales it like he hasn't eaten in days. His stomach begins to churn and make the same strange noises it did when he ate the ball. His entire body starts to lurch and convulse, until he finally opens his mouth wide and . . .

HORK!

"Holy trombolee! That is SO cool.

And look—they're made of glass, just like the lightbulb!"

I explain that Lightyear makes replicas of whatever he happens to see as he's eating, made of whatever substance he's eating. And he'll eat anything. Then I pull out a few of my other replica experiments to show Spotch and Rand-El. A toothbrush made of notebook paper. A Commander Virtue action figure made of picture frame metal and glass. A size 8 left-foot space boot made of synthesized macaroni and cheese.

We try a few more experiments, and then Rand-El abruptly changes the subject. "This is awesome, Kelv, and I almost hate to mention it, but have you come up with any ideas for getting us into your dad's lab to check out that robot? Remember, tonight is the only time everybody can make it."

Oh, I've thought about it. Pretty hard, in fact. And Mr. Smartest Kid in the Universe still hasn't come up with squat. "I don't know what to tell you, guys. Like I said, the only way into that lab is with a key card, and both my parents will be at Bula's art fair tonight. And they never leave the LIV space without those cards. In fact, they're heading out in about twenty minutes. I don't know what else to tell you. It's not like I have my own copy."

"I'll be right back," I say. "You guys look for something made of plastic."

Dad usually keeps his card on the entrance table when he's home, and I'm hoping that's where it is now. Yes! There it is! I snatch the card and head back toward my room.

"Just a minute there, young man. I think you know better than to try pulling something over on us."

It's Mom. Dang. I was so close.

"Your friends need to go home, Kelvin. Your father and I are leaving soon, and you know you can't have anyone over when we're not here."

"Oh . . . um . . . right. Sorry. I guess I lost track of the time. They'll be gone in five minutes, okay, Mom?"

"That's fine. And I'm sorry I jumped on you like that." Mom looks disappointed in herself. "I should know you wouldn't intentionally do something you're not supposed to."

Ugh. Moms really know how to hit you where it hurts. I know I shouldn't be doing this, but I really need to impress these guys somehow, and this is my chance. It's not like my Mighty Mega Supergeniusness has been knocking anybody out up to this point. I return to my room with the key card in hand. Spotch and Rand-El don't look too enthused.

"Did you find anything made of plastic?"

 "Well . . . kind of."

 "Wait, is that your . . ."

"Retainer. Yeah. It's the only thing we could find. We're not even sure if it's plastic. Maybe if we looked around a little more . . ."

"There's no time. You have to leave in a couple minutes. Sorry, but if we want to get into that lab tonight, this will have to do."

I hold the key card in front of Lightyear, and Rand-El gives him the retainer. I can't watch. Even Bula never put anything this disgusting in her mouth.

CHOMP-CHOMP!

HORK!

GALACTIC ACADEMY OF SCIENTISTS (G.A.S.)

Klyde Klosmo

Home planet: Earth

Species: Human

"This better work," Rand-El says. "I don't want crooked teeth for nothing."

"We'll find out soon enough," I say. "You guys get ahold of the others and tell them to meet us at the lift in thirty minutes."

Well, Mrs. Fuzzface, I see you managed to remove that teacup from the top of your head. Goody for you. And Miss Hairzy-bearzy's hind section is back below the table where it belongs. I suppose congratulations are in order.

Now leave me alone. I require total silence

as I concentrate on devising a plan to get myself into that blasted robot.

I SAID SILENCE! Wait. That must be Klosmo in the vacuu-suk 3000, getting himself ready for that awful art fair I overheard him yakking about. Ah . . . if only it would just suck him right out into space. Now that would be a glorious—ZARFLOOTS! THAT'S IT!

My diabolical brain just came up with a positively perfect plan, and I wasn't even trying very hard yet. And I need only wait until the klosmos leave for that feeble fair to put it into action!

30 minutes later . . .

At last. They're finally gone. Well, except for the boy. He's been holed up in his room for the past hour, though, so he shouldn't pose a problem. I just need to move quietly, which isn't particularly difficult when your feet are made of cotton.

Perfect! I can crawl through the air ducts to Klosmo's lab! You see, THIS is why I, Erik Failenheimer, will make such an excellent evil

universe ruler. my plan is utterly brilliant—
nothing can possibly go wrong. BWAHAHAHAHA!!!

okay, I guess something could go wrong.

Actually, this will make the trip to the lab much quicker. My brain must have known this and pushed the button on purpose. Without me even realizing it, my brilliant mind thinks of everything.

Okay, almost everything.

30

All right—time to go. Everything's lining up perfectly so far. The rest of the family should be gone for at least an hour and a half at Bula's preschool "art" fair. And I use the word "art" only because that's what the school is calling it. Here is Bula's entry:

The kids had to name their creation something fancy, just like in a real art show. Bula named hers Pony in a Sunny Meadow, which is odd, since I don't see a pony in there anywhere. Or a meadow. Or the sun. Chimp Scribbles would have been a better title, if you ask me. Not sure a chimp would agree, though. I'm just glad I could use tons of homework as an excuse not to go.

I have the retainer key card in my pocket, all dried off and ready. The rest of the gang should already be waiting at the elevator. This just better go smoothly. If we get caught sneaking around that lab, I'll be grounded for sure.

What the . . . ? That sounds like the Vacuu-Suk 3000. But I'm positive everybody left already. Maybe it's broken or something. I better check it out before I go.

I knock on the bathroom door, you know, just in case. No answer. "Mom?" I shout. "Is that you? Dad? Bula?" Still nothing. I crack open the door and peek inside. It's the Vacuu-Suk, all right, sucking away with no one inside. And one of the duct grates fell off and is lying on the floor. That's not good. Something could get sucked in there and clog everything up.

Maybe Lightyear got in here and accidentally turned it on. Whatever. I replace the grate and head for the front door.

31

Argh! I must have turned on the suction by mistake! How could I have been so stupid? It appears I'm really NOT as smart as the Klosmos. It appears all those years of second-place finishes were well deserved. It appears my position as janitor was completely appropriate after all. Egad—I can't bear to look!

And it appears I was wrong!

My brain must have sent out superintel-lect rays that shut the Vacuu-Suk 3000 fan down just as I was about to be sliced to bits! It's the only explanation! Zarfloots! If I'm this brilliant when I'm not even pay-ing attention, what chance will the universe have against an Erik Failenheimer who is actually focused and trying his best?

Off to the laboratory!

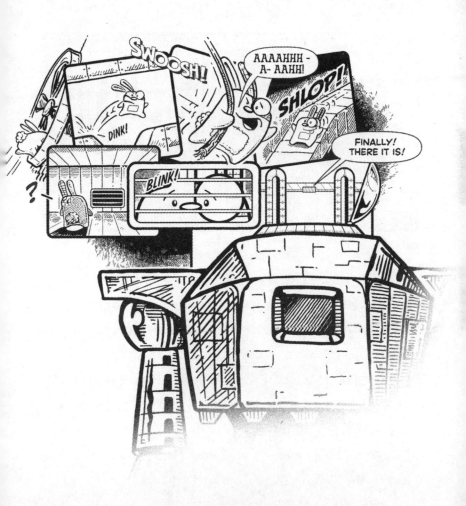

$\int$orry, boy, but this is strictly a nondog event. You'll just have to keep yourself busy for a couple hours. We'll play ball when I get back, though. I promise."

Wow, that's the most pathetic thing I've ever seen—if you don't count Bula's entry into the art fair. "Okay, Lightyear, you can come along," I tell him, against my better judgement. "But you better not eat anything."

I grab hold of Lightyear's leash and we head out the door. The hallway is empty. Good. If anybody does see me, I just need to play it cool, like everything is perfectly normal.

We're halfway to the end of the hallway when one of the other LIV-space doors opens. It's Mrs. Forzork, one of the cafeteria lunch ladies.

 **"Oh, hello, Kelvin. I thought I heard someone out here."**

"Hi, Mrs. F. I . . . uh . . . I was just taking my new dog for a walk. A perfectly normal walk. Down this perfectly normal hallway. In a perfectly normal way. Nothing odd going on here at all. No sirree.

And when I'm done, I'm heading straight back to my LIV space, without sneaking around or anything."

Nailed it!

"I see. Well, enjoy your perfectly normal walk, then. Oh, and make sure you get to the cafeteria early tomorrow—I'm whipping up a batch of my famous creamed blarf tongue, and it's sure to go fast."

"Will do, Mrs. F. And thanks for the heads-up!"

Yikes, that was a close one. This whole idea is getting worse by the minute. Well, at least I proved I can react well under pressure. Plus, I picked up a sweet tip on the blarf tongue. I'll make sure to pack my own lunch tomorrow.

Lightyear and I make our way around a few more turns, down a few more hallways, and finally reach the elevator.

HI, KELVIN!

"About time, Kelvin. What took you so long?"

"I ran into a little problem on the way here. Nothing I couldn't handle, though. It's really just a matter of staying cool, calm, and collected in the face of danger. I guess I just have a knack for it."

Oops. That won't go over well. Looks like it's time for some damage control.

"And that is an example of how *not* to stay cool, calm, and collected. I just wanted to demonstrate how not to react in case we run into any trouble on the way to the lab."

Hey! I think they're buying it!

 "Thanks, Kelv. Man, it's awesome having a genius in our group!"

"What about Brian?"

 "Oh—sorry, Brian. I meant someone who's always a genius."

Looks like I'm not the only one who's stressed out about this. Everybody's here, so we take the elevator down to the laboratory level. Fortunately, no one is working late and the hallways are empty. As we make our way toward my parents' lab, we pass the room that I remember seeing Lightyear in during our field trip visit. Looks like he remembers it, too.

So that's what he was licking up. I guess it all makes sense now. Well, at least as much sense as a space dog with a matter-duplicating stomach can make. We continue on to the large door at the end of the corridor . . . and the moment of truth.

It worked!

33

There it is, directly beneath me. Excellent! All I need to do is carefully loosen this grate and—

What in the name of peach cobbler is going on here? The levers are pointing the wrong way! The foot pedals are above my head! The gauges and control panels are upside down! Zarfloots!

Someone must have uncovered my diabolical plot to rule the universe. And that same someone must have altered the robot so I can't control it properly, in order to foil my plans. It's the only explanation!

well, that's a relief. I would hate to think I did all this nefarious evil planning for nothing.

And now for the truly brilliant part of my plan. The simpletons on this sorry excuse for a space station are simply going to open the door and let me walk out into space with the robot. But first things first.

And now the time has come to meet my

destiny. Farewell for now to all those who failed to give me my due, who mocked me, who celebrated my failures. The next time you gaze upon Erik Failenheimer, it will be from your knees as you beg for mercy! BWAHAHAHAHA!!!

34

hoa! I guess I didn't realize how humongous this lab really is when we were here earlier for the field trip. But now, with no one here working, it seems mighty mega super humongous. And quiet. Too quiet. It's really pretty darn creepy in here.

"Hey, guys," I say, "let's hurry up and do this. I need to be home before my parents get back from the art fair."

"Sure thing," says Rand-El. "This place is even more awesome than I remember. Your parents must be pretty awesome themselves to be in charge of all this."

Yeah, they must. My mom I guess I can understand, but who would have thought that my goofball of a dad was this important?

As we make our way over to the robot, we pass huge stacks of metal sheeting and Plexiglas. We pass bins filled with electronic parts and wiring, and shelves stacked with tools and hardware and space helmets of all shapes and sizes. There are also machines, big and small, to cut, bend, and shape the metal. You could build a battleship in here. Or a giant robot whose propulsion system we need to do a report on.

"Okay, I'm pretty sure the propulsion system is in the feet, so let's start there."

"Just be careful. And don't touch anything."

"Sure. And then we can write a report based on staring at a giant metal foot. That should land us a pretty sweet grade."

"Hey! There's some kind of access panel on the back of the foot. Let's take a look inside."

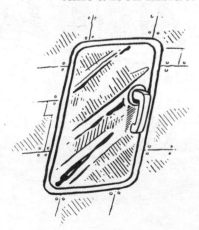

"Uh . . . I don't think that's a good idea."

 "C'mon, Kelv. It's a great idea. What's the problem? If we aren't even going to check this thing out, what was the point of sneaking in here in the first place?"

My thoughts exactly. My only goal now is getting back to the LIV space without getting caught, which seems less likely by the minute.

 "What's that? Who touched something they weren't supposed to?"

"No, that's not it. Look! It's the robot's dome! It's starting to close!"

"What the heck is going on?"

"The station is going through the fire drill protocol."

 "But doesn't that mean—"

"Yup. The inner doors are sealed and we're stuck in here."

 "But doesn't that also mean—"

"Yup. The outer air lock doors are going to open up and suck all the oxygen out of the lab."

 "But that means—"

"Yup. We'll be sucked out into space right along with the oxygen."

Suddenly I'm not so worried about being

grounded anymore. I glance around the lab in a panic and notice Mippitt at one of the storage shelves. He's holding a helmet in each hand.

"Quick, everybody—take a helmet! And grab on to something heavy so we don't get sucked out the air lock when it opens!"

I look around frantically for something to grab hold of. Mippitt is waving us over to the giant

robot, where he has his arm locked around the access door handle on the back of the foot. Yes!

 "Head for the robot! There's no way that gigantic hunk of metal is being sucked out the air lock."

The rest of us hurry over to Mippitt just as the enormous air lock doors begin to open. The problem, besides the fact that we're seconds from being sucked out into the vast darkness of space, is that there's only one handle.

Hey! This just might work, as long as the air lock doesn't stay open too long! The pull toward the open doors is getting stronger, but everyone seems to be holding on okay. And the robot hasn't budged! The only way this massive piece of metal is going out those doors is if it decides to walk over there itself!

This is NOT good. I don't get it—the robot just up and walked off the space station! Like . . . on purpose! At least Mippitt showed us where to press on our belts in order to pressurize our uniforms. They're made of a special thermal material, too, but they won't keep us warm out here for long. We have to do something fast before we turn into spacesicles! Although that would keep us from suffocating, since our helmets produce only about four hours of oxygen.

Uh-oh. Mippitt is having trouble with that handle. It looks like he's losing his grip! If he goes, we all go! No—wait! The access door! With my brain being distracted by thoughts of drifting aimlessly in space for the rest of my life, I completely forgot about it! He's trying to get it open!

I pull myself forward next to Mippitt and grab hold of the handle. We pull with everything we've got, but the door won't budge. I signal for Grimnee to join us up front and tell her what we're trying to do. If she can't pry that thing open, nobody can. She yanks on the door with everything she's got.

Nothing.

This is bad.

I can feel the cold beginning to make its way through my suit. Lightyear must really be feeling it. He doesn't even have a suit. His fur must be a pretty good insulator, though, because he's hanging in there. And what's really weird—he doesn't even seem to need oxygen, which is good, seeing as we forgot to get him a helmet. None of this matters, though, if we can't get inside that robot. The way I see it, we have one more shot.

"Hey, Grimnee," I say through the intercom in our helmets. "That access door is being a bit of a bully, don't you think? Making us stay out here in the cold and all?"

Problem solved. We pull ourselves into the robot's boot and shut the door that Grimnee tore open behind us. There's a lot of room, but we stick close together. Everybody is pretty shaken up. Gil's water globe is frozen solid, so we roll him over to a pipe that's giving off a lot of heat so he can thaw out.

It's loud in here, since the propulsion system runs through the boot. It's also warm, though, so nobody is complaining. I lift my head and can see right up the inside of the robot's leg. There are pipes and ducts and electronic panels and ladders and catwalks all over the place. I still can't believe my dad designed this thing.

 "I thought you said this robot was too heavy to be sucked out the air lock. Now what are we supposed to do?"

"C'mon, Rand-El. It didn't get sucked out. It walked out. You saw it. We all did."

 "Yeah, well, that doesn't make any sense."

 "Maybe your mom and dad did that thing. You know, where they put someone's mind into the robot?"

"I don't think so. My mom said they hadn't even tested the mind-transfer beam yet. They were going to run some experiments on smaller stuff before they tried it on any of the robots."

"Smaller stuff? You mean like a toaster? Were they going to transfer someone's mind into a toaster, Kelvin? That would be great, you know. Then I could just tell it to make my toast darker instead of changing the setting. Just think of the time I could save if I didn't have to—"

"Knock it off, Rand-El. Look, we're all a little panicky right now."

"A little panicky? A LITTLE?! We've

been sucked out into space, in the middle of nowhere, stuck in a robot foot, headed for who knows where, with no way to tell anybody what happened! I'm a lot panicky right now, Kelv. A LOT!"

"Well, somebody must be up in this thing's head controlling it. Maybe they're just taking it out for a test flight or something. It looks like these ladders might go all the way to the top. Somebody should climb up and take a look."

"I'll go! I used to climb stuff way higher than this back home."

"After what we saw in Coach Ed's class, I don't doubt it. Be careful, though. And don't let whoever is driving this thing see you—we

have no idea what they might be

up to."

Am I one heck of an evil genius, or what? I said they would open the door and let me walk right out, and that's just what they did!

All I had to do was use a little laser to set fire to a bin filled with electronic equipment. Galactic Academy of Scientists, my fuzzy-tailed behind. More like the Galactic Academy of Simpletons!

I should be arriving at the planetoid shortly. Once Zurton is in view, I'll use the robot's energy detection scanner to locate the all-powerful Zorb. And because my new plushy body's not actually alive, it can't harm me!

Zarfloots! It's great to be me!

They thought I wasn't worthy of being on their scientific team—that I wasn't as smart as they were. And yet here I am, so close to achieving my diabolical goal I can taste it! And it tastes GOOD! Like baked beans! With little cut-up hot dog pieces in it. And a squirt of mustard on top.

Soon, very soon, the universe will be mine to command. And I will have all the baked beans my evil heart desires!

There's a scuffling sound from just out of sight. It's Zot. She's on her way back down. When she gets to about the tenth ladder rung from the bottom, she jumps off, does a flip, and lands in the middle of the rest of us.

"Well?" Gil asks. "What did you find out?"

Zot tells us what she over heard about the Zorb. And how we'll all die if we get too close to it. And that whoever is driving the robot intends to get VERY close to it. Super. Why doesn't an asteroid just land on our heads while we're at it?

"And it sounds like he's planning to use the Zorb to take over the universe," she adds.

"So it's a he?" I ask.

Zot thinks it over for a second. "Well, it sure sounded like a he. But if there's one thing I've learned since I've been on the space station, it's to never take anything for granted."

Don't I know it.

"This is bad. REAL BAD! Why did I ever let Kelvin talk me into sneaking into the lab in the first place?"

 "What? This was all your idea, Rand-El. I was happy to just stay home tonight and play with Lightyear."

 "Well, that's not how I remember it. Not that it matters. It sounds like we'll all be dead in a few minutes anyway."

 "We'll be just fine. Or did you forget—we happen to have Kelvin with us. He'll think of something to get us out of this mess. Right, Kelv?"

 "Uhh . . . about that . . . "

 "In fact, he probably already did."

"Well, I . . ."

"I mean, there's NO WAY the smartest kid in the entire universe is going to let his pals die a horrible and gruesome death, am I right?"

That's it! I can't take it anymore. If this is the end, then there's no way I'm going down lying to these guys. And if that means they don't respect me anymore, fine. If they only liked me in the first place because they thought I was smart, so be it. It's not like I'll have to spend much time being friendless anyway, the way things are going.

"Okay, look, everybody—I've got a confession to make. I'm not really a Mighty Mega Supergenius. I mean, I hope to be someday— I expect it to kick in at some point, but it definitely hasn't yet. And I'm really sorry for leading everybody on since I got here. And I understand if you all hate me for lying about it. I wanted to tell you all sooner, but the whole thing just kept growing and growing and turned into such a big deal that I was too embarrassed to let the cat out of the bag."

 "Ha, ha! Kelvin are not smart!"

 "Hey, that's all right, Kelvin. Heck, I might not be as handsome as I think I am, either."

 "Definitely not. And there's no way Zot can be as peppy and cheerful as she tries to make us all believe."

"Okay. Bad example."

 "Wait a minute! This is all real sweet and everything, but with Kelvin turning out to be a dud in the smarts department—"

 "I wouldn't say 'dud,' exactly—"

 "Whatever. The point is, who the heck is going to get us out of this mess now?!"

 "Yeah! Rand-El is right! When this robot lands near the Zorb, we're all going to turn to goo. I don't want to turn to goo. I'm a strictly non-goo kind of guy!"

 "I don't know. It might be kind of fun! Well, except for the being-dead part, I mean."

I guess they really were counting on me to get us out of this jam. And why wouldn't they? I was the smartest kid in the universe, after all. With that out the door, though, everybody's starting to lose it.

"All right," I say, "let's try not to panic. We need to take this one step at a time. And the first thing we need to do is make sure this robot doesn't land anywhere near that Zorb."

Rand-El looks at me with scrunched eyebrows. All six of them.

"And just how are we supposed to do that, Mr. Genius?"

And that's what I was afraid of. Although the "Mr." part was a nice touch.

"I don't know," I say. "But I know someone who does."

"And who might that be?" Rand-El asks, his eyebrows scrunching even more.

"Him," I say, pointing toward the corner.

Rand-El looks confused. "Brian?" he says. "You mean the guy playing twiddly toes over there? He's going to get us out of this mess?"

"Sure," I say, "we just need to calm him down so his brain grows."

Now Rand-El looks more mad than confused. "Calm him down? Out here? Brian gets stressed out when he has to pick between regular and low-fat snorge slices at lunch!"

"We have to take his mind off the situation," I say. "Can anybody sing?"

Zot leaps to her feet. "Grimnee can! She's great! She was the choir in the talent show last month!"

"You mean she was *in* the choir," I tell her.

"No! She was the whole thing!"

Grimnee jumps to her feet.

LA-LA-LA-
LAHHHHHHHHH...

Even with her helmet on, she sounds fantastic. It's like a whole bunch of voices are coming out of the same mouth.

"How does she do that?" I ask Zot.

"She told me she has four throats. She can even eat and sing at the same time. When she has a cough, though, you do not want to be anywhere close."

It seems to be working! Brian is just staring at Grimnee, and his brain is beginning to pulse. And grow. I never really watched too closely before. It's pretty gross. When his brain has grown to the point that it completely fills his dome, Brian speaks.

"We need to disrupt the robot's propulsion system and force it into an emergency landing. The odds that we'll be far enough from the Zorb to remain safe are extremely high."

"Oh yeah?" Zot says. "How high?"

"About thirteen percent," answers Brian.

Zot looks confused. "Only THIRTEEN PERCENT!"

Brian grins. "Just kidding," he says. "I thought the mood needed a little lightening up around here. The odds are actually closer to ninety-three percent."

I walk over to Gil's bubble. "You see that electronics panel over there?"

"Yeah," he says. "What about it?"

"Get it wet. That should shut down the propulsion system in this entire leg."

Now it's Spotch who looks confused. "Wait a minute," he says. "I thought you said you weren't that smart."

"Well, I'm smart enough to read that sign," I say.

Gil looks excited. "Okay. I'm on it!"

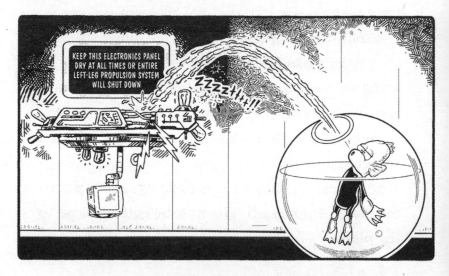

The huge thrust cylinder in the robot's leg begins to shudder. Then sputter. And then it stops completely. It worked!

Brian nods his enormous-brained head approvingly. "Nicely done! There should still be enough control left with the right-leg propulsion unit for the robot to make a somewhat safe emergency landing on the planetoid."

"Somewhat safe?" Rand-El asks.

"Eighty-seven percent chance," Brian answers.

With only one leg thruster working, the robot's flight becomes very unsteady. We're having a tough time keeping our balance. Well, except for Zot.

Another idea pops into my head, and I stumble over to Brian to bounce it off him. He nods again, and this time the enormous weight of his brain nearly makes him topple over. Once he regains his balance, he heads off toward a huge junction of switches and cables.

A red emergency light is flashing, and a warning alarm is going off. We must be getting close to the planetoid.

"Okay, everybody," I shout over the noise, "when we touch down, we need to get out of here right away and find cover."

A third idea just popped into my head.

THERE IT IS! ZURTON!

And sitting somewhere on its surface is the zorb! I should be close enough now to pinpoint its exact location.

I probably shouldn't say this, because I've been burned before, but—no! I better not. Best to wait until I actually have the zorb in my possession this time before I get all braggy and full of myself. Surely I can hold it in another few minutes and then . . . and then . . . AHH, THE HECK WITH IT!

I am about to become the most powerful being in the universe, and (don't do it, you're just asking for trouble) NOTHING CAN STOP ME! BWAHAHAHA!!!

Why me?! Seriously, is it really asking all that much to become an all-powerful being and rule the entire universe?

How did this happen? All systems were go when I left the space station. It just doesn't make any sense! Somebody out there must not like me.

And yet, all may not be lost! If I can manage an emergency landing on Zurton without causing too much damage to the robot, I should still be able to make it to the Zorb. Even if this robot has to crawl to get there. And then NOTHING WILL STOP M—good gravy! Will I never learn? Seriously, what is wrong with me?

Uh-oh. The planetoid is coming on fast! It will require every last ounce of my diabolical brilliance to make this work! It will take all the fiendish cunning I can muster to safely stick this landing!

Or I suppose I could push that button over there.

It's working! The robot is nearly on the ground. Just a hundred feet more. Fifty. Ten. Touchdown!

What madness is this?! Those appear to be children! And if I'm not mistaken, one of them is . . . no! It can't be! It's that Klosmo boy! He must be the one who sabotaged my robot! Well, I know one member of that infuriating family that will never interfere with my plans again!

The robot's mobility system needs a few minutes to reboot. But then those helmeted hooligans will wish they had never crossed paths with Erik Failenheimer.

Ten minutes later . . .

That will teach you to interfere with the universe-conquering plans of Erik Failenheimer! BWAHAHAHA!!!

Once I retrieve the Zorb, perhaps, PERHAPS, I'll come back and free the little doofuses. They can have the privilege of being the first to kneel before my awesome might.

The scanner says the Zorb is up on that distant plateau. I'm so excited I think I'll run!

 "Whoa! That could have been us under all that rubble!"

"As long as whoever is in that robot thinks it was, we should be okay for now."

"Good boy, Lightyear! Those copies of us were spot on."

"Are you okay, Lightyear? It looked like you were having a little trouble spitting out that Grimnee look-alike."

"Yeah, I think he'll be fine. But I can't believe he ate that much rock in that short of a time."

PANT PANT PANT

We were lucky to get out of that mess, but now we have even bigger problems. No one back at the space station knows where we are. Our oxygen supply won't last forever. And then there's still that little issue of a maniac in a giant robot who wants to rule the universe.

"It's great that we disabled the thruster and all," Rand-El says, "but that robot can still walk over and grab that energy thingy without it. As a matter of fact, look over there!"

We all look in the direction Rand-El is pointing. Then we all squint in the direction Rand-El is pointing. Gil finally says what we're all thinking.

"I don't see anything."

None of us do. But none of us have the long-distance vision of Rand-El's top set of eyes, either.

"Well, I can see him. He's about ten miles away and he's running toward that plateau."

"Just keep watching," says Brian, "and let us know what happens. Kelvin and I left him a little surprise."

Rand-El climbs onto a nearby rock to get a better view. "Okay," he says, "the robot has reached the plateau. Now it's climbing up the side. It's on top now, and I can see a glow coming from the ground in front of him."

 "It must be that Zorp thing, or whatever it's called."

"And now it's reaching for the Zorf! That's just great! We're all doomed!"

"Keep watching."

 "What the heck? The robot just blasted off into space! Without the Zork!"

"Excellent," Brian says. "Before we fled from

the robot, Kelvin had me set the propulsion system in the right leg to turn on after a brief period, run for thirty minutes, and then shut down. Forever."

"Wait a minute," says Zot. "If you could control the leg thruster, why didn't you just fly us back to the space station?"

"All I could do from the boot was set the thruster to turn on and off at specific intervals. There weren't any controls. And it wouldn't have mattered anyway. With only one thruster operational, there is no way to control the robot's flight from the command dome, either. Our would-be universe conqueror will spend the rest of his days drifting aimlessly through space in a busted-up robot."

Busted up?

"Without having nothin' to do or anything."

What's going on here?

"I like pancakes."

Oh, right. Grimnee stopped singing a little while ago, so Brian must be stressing out again. Not that it really matters. Even brilliant Brian wouldn't be able to help us now.

"Hey, Grimnee. Start singing again. We need smart Brian to get us off this stupid planetoid."

"What's the point? Unless his brain suddenly sprouts thrusters, there's nothing he can do to get us back home. Let's face it—we're stuck here!"

"Stuck here? We can't be stuck here! I have homework corrections to turn in to Ms. Gassias tomorrow or I lose half a point. A WHOLE HALF A POINT!"

"Don't worry about it, Gil. You'll have an excuse."

"I will? What?"

"You'll be dead."

"He'll need a note for that."

"Hey, guys, cheer up! We DID save the universe, you know. And quintillions of living beings. Kelvin, you might not be a genius, but you sure came through under pressure."

Yeah, I guess so. But it wasn't just me.

"Thanks, but everybody did their part to help out. Even Lightyear. I might not be a Mighty Mega Supergenius—yet—but together I think we proved we're even better. I mean, Zot's right—we just saved the universe!"

 "Yeah, that's great and all. But it doesn't change the fact that we're still stuck on this planetoid! And

running out of oxygen! And no one even knows we're here!"

Leave it to Rand-El to bring us back to reality. But he's right. I can't believe this is happening. I travel halfway across the galaxy to start a new life, make a bunch of new friends, and don't even make it to my second week? And what about all that effort I wasted pretending to be something I'm not? Why? What does it matter now? And then there's Mom and Dad. I lied to them, too, and let them believe I was a genius. And now I'm never going to see them again. They'll never know the truth. Jeez, I miss them already. I'd even be happy to see Bula right now.

Zot screams. "What the heck is THAT?!"

Spotch stumbles backward, away from the creature's shadow. "I don't know, but I don't think oxygen is our biggest problem right now!"

Grimnee, who was sitting against one of the smaller rocks, leaps to her feet. She slides in front of us and stands her ground. She's making the same growling sound she did just before mashing Dorn into that wad of desks in Ms. Gassias's class. Grimnee hates bullies.

"What the . . . ?" I say, dumbfounded. "Bula?! How did you get here?!"

"DAD!" I yell as I run over to give him the biggest hug of my life.

"But . . . how did you even know we were here?" I ask.

Dad points to Mippitt. "He told me."

"Mippitt?" I say. "But . . . how? He doesn't even talk."

"Heck, he's not even really a HE. Mippitt is a robot. I built him to keep an eye on you while you got used to your new school. Once you landed on this planetoid, Mippitt contacted us to report your situation. He actually has quite a sophisticated communication system. Strictly nonverbal, though. Don't tell your mother, or she'll want to install the same thing on me. HAR! Anyway, as soon as he relayed your coordinates, Bula and I jumped in a shuttle and hurried right on over. Boy, a few miles closer to that Zorb and you guys would all be puddles of goo right now."

Brian looks excited. "I like goo!"

"Sorry for keeping Mippitt a secret, Kelvin, but we thought it was for your own good. We just wanted to help keep you safe."

Safe? Wait until he hears the whole story of our group's little excursion to his lab. But first I have something more important to get off my chest.

"Since we're giving away secrets, I've got one for you. And I'm really sorry about it. I'm a phony, Dad. I've been pretending to be a Mighty Mega Supergenius, but I'm really only about average, intelligence-wise."

"If that," chirps Rand-El.

"But everyone expects me to be more than that because you and Mom are so smart. Sometimes I think that's the only reason other kids even like me. And I didn't want to let anyone down, you know? Especially you guys. I just wanted you to be proud of me."

"Proud of you?" Dad says. "Kelvin, your mom and I are super proud of you. And it has nothing to do with how smart you are—although I think you might be selling yourself short there. You never know when geniusness might kick in."

"That's exactly what I keep telling myself!"

Dad leans in closer. "You want to hear another secret? We knew you weren't a Mighty Mega Supergenius."

"You did? How?"

"Well, son, the D+ in geometry last year was a pretty big clue. HAR! But we were happy to go along with it if that's what you wanted. In fact, I even programmed Mippitt to help you keep up the illusion until you finally decided to come clean."

The rest of the gang has been hooting and hollering and dancing around in circles since Dad showed up. But now they're getting impatient. Spotch points to his helmet and says, "My low-oxygen-level warning is starting to flash. Do you think we could make our way to the shuttle?"

"Yeah," Rand-El adds, "we're all real proud of you, Kelvin. And if we're still breathing in five minutes, we'll be even prouder."

We head over to the shuttle and everyone hops in. And on the way back home we tell Dad the story of how we saved the universe.

Epilogue

Three weeks later . . .

I just HAD to do it. There I am, the zorb mere feet from my grasp, the universe moments from being mine to command, and what do I say?

"NOTHING CAN STOP ME NOW!"

What a moron.

So now I'm left floating helplessly through the lonely depths of space forever. Without a book or anything. All this evil brilliance—WASTED!

What the . . . ?

It appears I have collided with an asteroid of some sort! Not that that will help me any—I'm still drifting aimlessly through space. But, hey, at least now I can leave the robot and run around and get a little exercise. I could even live in one of the craters or something. Better yet, I could use the robot's lasers to fashion a castle of sorts from this rock.

Yes! That's it! I will control it all! I will become the evil ruler of this entire asteroid! NOTHING CAN STOP ME NOW! BWAHAHAH—

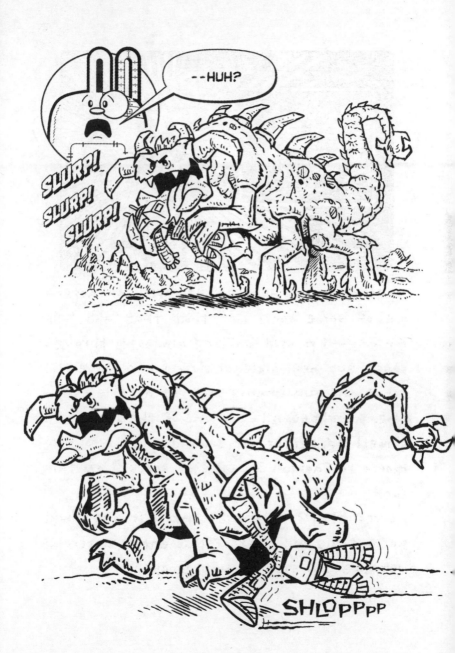

Acknowledgments

A big shout out to the preposterously patient Dan Lazar, seriously sensational Cecilia de la Campa, and all the great folks at Writers House. You guys always come through.

A huge heaping helping of gratitude to James Patterson, Reagan Arthur, and Jenny Bak for making *Sci-Fi Junior High* the first outside acquisition for Jimmy Patterson Books. It is truly an honour.

A plentiful portion of appreciation to Aubrey Poole and Tracy Shaw for lending their skill, creativity, and attention to detail to the project. The book is better because of you.

About the Authors

John Martin is the illustrator of the Vordak the Incomprehensible series. A day doesn't go by without him drawing monsters, robots, and characters from his childhood. He lives in Michigan with his wife, Mary; sons, Adam and Paul; and daughter, Grace.

Scott Seegert is the author of the Vordak the Incomprehensible series. If you didn't know better, and couldn't see him, you would swear he was twelve years old. He lives in Michigan with his wife, Margie; sons, Brad and Jason; and daughter, Shannon.

The Adventure Continues

2018